THE TRAVELS OF

Ermine

The World Tour

D0711633

 By Jennifer Gray ★ Illustrated by Elisa Paganelli

 USBORNE

THE TRAVELS OF Ermine

The World Tour

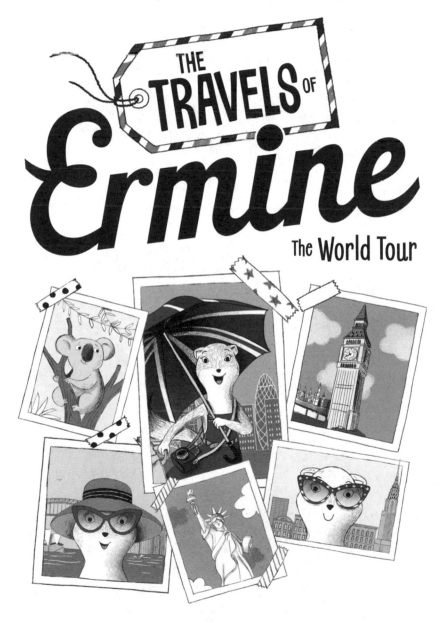

THE TRAVELS OF

Ermine

Contents

Trouble in New York

SYDNEY
★ ★ ★
POSTAGE

LONDON · LONDON

THE TRAVELS OF

Ermine

Trouble in New York

How to make a travel

Ermine loves sticking photos, tickets, maps, postcards and more in her scrapbook as a way of remembering all the fabulous places she's visited. Why not give it a try yourself?

Step 1: Choose your scrapbook

Choosing the right scrapbook is very important. Think about how big you want it to be, what you might want on the cover, and what sort of paper you'd like.

Ermine's top tip:
I love the smell of a new scrapbook, and I even chose a shiny ribbon to go around mine!

Step 2: Find your memories

Once you've found your scrapbook, it's time to start collecting. You can put anything in a travel scrapbook. Tickets? Check! Photos? Check! A leaf from a park you've visited? Check!

scrapbook like Ermine

EXTRA-STICKY GLUE

Step 3: Stick it down

Now you're happy with the layout of your page, it's time to start gluing!

Ermine's top tip:

I always leave my pages to dry out before closing my scrapbook.

NEW YORK

very big TEETH!

Step 4: Travel!

Decide where you want to travel to next...

Ermine's top tip:

I love to explore – from new countries and cities, to my own home, the outdoors, indoors and anywhere else I fancy. All you need is a dash of determination, a sprinkle of courage, and a dollop of curiosity!

Ermine's top tip:

I always place everything on the page first, so I can move things around and make sure I'm happy with how it looks!

Happy travels!

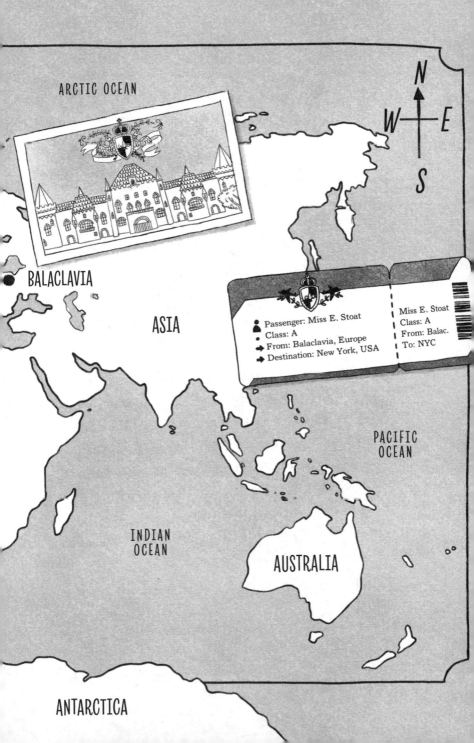

Dear Michael,

I am writing to tell you that I have recently adopted a very determined young lady named Ermine and I am sending her on a trip to see the world. New York City seems like a good place to start, so I have given her your address and told her to look you up. I am sure you will take care of her and show her the sights. She will be arriving next Wednesday afternoon.

Please send my regards to the former Mrs. Megabucks and say hello to Mike Junior for me.

With best wishes,

Maria. Grand Duchess Maria Von Schnitzel

OPEN LETTER

Michael S. Megabucks

Megabucks Bank

123 Wall Street

Mew York NY10005

Chapter 1

Manhattan, NYC...

Michael S. Megabucks sat at his mega-desk in his mega-office drinking a mega-cup of coffee. The office was at the top of a mega-building overlooking the mega-skyline of Manhattan in New York City.

Megabucks Bank was located in one of the tallest skyscrapers in the city and the bird's-eye view of the glittering glass buildings was spectacular, especially in the winter sunshine. Michael S. Megabucks never tired of it.

He swiveled round and round in his leather chair to take another look.

"Excuse me, Mr. Megabucks." His assistant poked his head around the door.

"Whadisit, Sam?" Michael S. Megabucks scowled.

"There's someone here to see you, Sir."

"I thought I told ya to keep this afternoon free." Michael S. Megabucks had one son – Mike Junior. Today was Mike Junior's eighth birthday and he had something special planned.

"I'm real sorry, Sir," said the assistant, running his fingers through his hair. "I've told her to come back tomorrow but she just won't take no for an answer. She says you're expecting her." He raised his eyebrows.

"Something about a postcard…from a duchess?"

"Oh, shoot!" Michael S. Megabucks said. "I'd forgotten all about that. You'd better send the young lady in."

"Thank you, Sir."

Michael S. Megabucks heard a scampering sound on the corridor's marble floor. "Hey!" he yelled after the assistant. "Did she bring a dog?"

"No, Sir," the assistant called. "She's alone."

"What's that scratching noise then?"

The assistant didn't reply. Instead he popped his head back around the mega-door and announced, "Miss Ermine, Sir."

A small, snow-white, furry animal with a long bushy tail, two coal-black eyes, white whiskers and a pink nose trotted into the room.

She was wearing a blue pinafore dress and a woolly scarf, and stood about half as high as his knee. A camera was slung over her shoulder and in one paw she carried a small bag marked TOOL BAG. She leaped up onto the desk.

"Hello," she said, "you must be Mike Senior." She removed a tattered photograph from her dress pocket and regarded him closely. "Although you're rather *different* from what I was expecting."

Michael S. Megabucks blushed.

He and the Duchess

were old friends. It had been quite a while since he'd seen her, but he didn't think he'd changed *that* much. "*You're* Ermine?" he said, looking at her doubtfully. "Maria didn't say anything about a *weasel*."

Ermine gave him a frosty look. Her whiskers twitched. "I am NOT a weasel!" she said sternly. "I'm a stoat."

"What's the difference?" Michael S. Megabucks said.

"*What's the difference?*" Ermine spluttered. "I turn white in the winter and brown in the summer, for one. And I have a black tip on the end of my tail –" she waved it in his direction so he could see – "and I'm far cleverer. I live a lot longer too, so I've got lots and lots and *lots* of relatives."

Michael S. Megabucks decided to change the subject.

He didn't want Ermine's entire family descending on him from Balaclavia. "How d'ya know Maria?" he asked instead.

"The Duke wanted to use me to trim the collar of his robe," Ermine explained. "You know – the one he wore in the old days when he went to see the King."

"Ah," said Michael S. Megabucks. He was dimly aware that Balaclavia no longer had a king and as a result the Duke and Duchess had fallen on hard times.

"The Duke still uses it for dressing up," Ermine told him. "He keeps it in a trunk at the castle, only the fur collar got moldy because the castle roof was leaking. The Duchess told him to replace it with velvet instead but he set a trap to catch me anyway.

It's very precious, you know – my white fur. It's called ermine, like me." She let out a deep, shuddering sigh. "Can you believe that some people want to sew it onto *clothes*?"

"Terrible," Michael S. Megabucks agreed.

"Luckily the Duchess came to the rescue," Ermine continued. "She told the Duke that the only place for ermine is on a stoat. Then she adopted me. She's taught me lots of useful things, like how to use a wrench and when to wear a feathered hat. And now she's sent me on a trip around the world to complete my education."

"Good for her," said Michael S. Megabucks. "That sounds like Maria!" An idea occurred to him. "Say, whaddya think about coming to meet my kid?"

Ermine looked confused. "The Duchess

never mentioned you kept baby goats."

Michael S. Megabucks guffawed. "I mean my son – Mike Junior. It's his birthday today and I got something planned. You can stay over a couple of days at the apartment if you like. Mike Junior can show ya around the city."

"Oh, I'm staying much longer than that," Ermine replied brightly. "The Duchess says I can't leave until I've filled up my scrapbook. That could take weeks."

Michael S. Megabucks opened his mouth to say something, then closed it again as

a thought occurred to him. As well as it being his birthday, Mike Junior had the Christmas vacation coming up and he was due to stay for a while. The kid was always asking if he could have a pet. Sure, what Mike Junior really wanted was an alligator, but a talking stoat wasn't a bad substitute.

"Great!" Michael S. Megabucks grabbed his coat. "We'll be glad to have ya." He looked at the tool bag. "Is that all the luggage you got?"

Ermine shook with laughter. "Of course it isn't, silly! I mean would *you* travel the world with just a tool bag?"

"I suppose not," Michael S. Megabucks admitted.

"I always carry it with me, in case there's an emergency," Ermine said. "The rest of my bags are at the airport at the Baggage Office."

"I'll get Sam to send someone for them right away," said Michael S. Megabucks.

Ermine jumped onto his shoulder and waved her tool bag in the direction of the door. "What are we waiting for then? Let's go and meet Mike Junior."

Ermine's whiskers twitched in excitement.

Her TRAVELS had truly begun!

Chapter 2

Meanwhile at the airport...

Two men in overcoats sat in a coffee shop in the arrivals terminal. One was short and fat with a tattoo across his knuckles and a false beard. The other was tall and slim with slicked-back hair and a pair of dark glasses. They had chosen a corner table away from other customers so they wouldn't be seen.

The tall one picked up
a discarded newspaper
and began to read.

New York Breaking News

SPUDD BROTHERS ESCAPE FROM PRISON!

Mystery of famous Toffany Diamond remains unsolved!

REWARD OFFERED FOR INFORMATION!

"You sure the cops aren't onto us?" the short one whispered.

The tall one peered out from behind his paper. Apart from a couple of routine security guards patrolling the busy concourse, the coast was clear. "Relax," he said. "No one suspects a thing." He glared at the other man. "Though you'd better put your gloves on in case anyone sees your tattoo."

"Why?" said the other.

"Because it spells your name, you idiot."

"Oh yeah. Sorry, Harry."

Barry pulled on a tiny pair of baby-pink woolly gloves. He had made them at the knitting class in prison.

"Why'd you have to choose those?" Harry snarled. "D'you want everyone looking at you?"

Barry looked hurt. "I like pink," he said. "And anyway, I ran out of yarn."

"I don't see why you got that tattoo in the first place," his brother grumbled. "I mean it's pretty dumb having your name tattooed on your knuckles when you're a robber."

"The prison guard said it was a good idea," Barry protested.

"Sure he did." Harry sighed. He checked around to see if anyone was looking, put on his hat and stood up. "Now let's get that diamond

29

back from its hiding place." He strode off in the direction of the Baggage Office.

Barry hurried after him. His short legs made it difficult to keep up. "You certain it'll still be there?" he panted.

Harry patted him on the head. "Of course it'll still be there. You saw the paper. If anyone else had found the diamond, it wouldn't be a mystery any more, would it?"

The two men approached the counter cautiously. The attendant didn't look up. He was collecting a very large number of very small cases of assorted colors from the store behind the counter and piling them onto a cart.

"Ahem," said Harry.

"Be with you in a minute," the attendant said.

Barry leaned over. "That's a lot of bags," he observed.

"Yeah, they're the property of a passenger by the name of Miss E. Stoat," the attendant replied. "Flew in from Balaclavia earlier today. Someone's just come to pick them up for her."

BAGGAGE

"Stoat?" Barry said. "That's an unusual name."

"You could say!" The attendant chuckled. "Kinda suits her though, from what I could see."

"How come?" Barry asked. He liked chatting with people. In fact, that was how the Spudd Brothers had ended up in prison – because Barry couldn't keep his mouth shut.

"It doesn't matter!" Harry growled. Any minute now Barry would be telling the attendant his life story, including the part about them breaking out of jail and coming to the airport to retrieve a stolen diamond from the Baggage Office. In fact it was only by not telling his brother anything about where the diamond was hidden until that morning that Harry had managed to keep it a secret for so long.

The attendant placed one more bag on the pile. He beckoned to the courier who was standing nearby. "Okay, that's all of it," he said. "You can take them now."

The courier disappeared with the cart towards the exit.

"Now what can I do for you gentlemen?" said the attendant, giving them his full attention.

"We're here to pick up a package," Harry said.

"Got a ticket?" the attendant asked.

"Yeah." Harry reached into his pocket and handed him a moldy luggage claim ticket.

The attendant frowned. "This looks years old."

"We've been away…" Barry began.

"On vacation," said Harry quickly.

"Anywhere nice?" asked the attendant.

Barry opened his mouth to reply but Harry cut him off. "It was okay," he said. "The rooms were a little small." He wished the attendant would stop asking questions.

"Aw, I don't know – they weren't bad for a prison," Barry said.

Harry gave his brother a kick. "He means hotel," he said. "It's just his sense of humor."

"Funny." The attendant rummaged around in the office. Then he handed Harry a small leather case with a metal clasp and a fancy handle. "Here you are."

"You sure that's the one?" Harry asked, examining the case. It was so long since he'd left it there it was hard to remember exactly what it had looked like, apart from the fact it was dark blue. "Shouldn't it have a ticket?"

"This was on the floor next to it." The attendant held out a yellowing ticket stub and compared it with the one Harry had given him. "See, the number matches."

Harry examined the two tickets. It certainly seemed like it was the right case.

"Why don't you open it and check everything's there, just to be on the safe side?" the attendant suggested.

"That's a good idea, Harry," said Barry.

"No, it's not!" Harry poked him hard in the ribs with his elbow. He tucked the little case under his coat. "And my name's not Harry, it's…ah… Harri-et. See you around."

He grabbed Barry's arm and pulled him in the direction of the elevator.

Once inside, Harry pushed the button for the top floor of the parking lot.

The door opened. They made for their clapped-out old clunker of a car.

"That's a good idea, Harry!" Harry mimicked as they jumped into the car and slammed the doors. "Are you a complete dope? What if he'd seen the diamond? And why did you have to tell him my name?"

"Sorry." Barry looked crestfallen. "I think you covered it pretty well though.

You kind of suit Harriet." He made a grab for the case but Harry shook him off.

"It was my idea to hide it there, so I get to open it." He raised the little leather case to his lips and kissed it. Then he wrinkled his nose and sniffed. A musky smell was coming from within.

"What's the matter?" Barry said.

"Smells like those ferrets Grandma Spudd used to keep in her drawer." Harry took another sniff and shrugged. "Must be because it's been there so long." He snapped open the clasp. "Feast your eyes, brother. We're finally gonna be rich. This is our ticket to a new life."

"Yeah – Hawaii here we come!" Barry leaned over expectantly.

Harry lifted the lid. Both men gasped. Inside the case was a small, feathered hat.

Chapter 3

Back in New York City...

Ermine sat on Michael S. Megabucks's
shoulder as they traveled along the wide
avenues of Manhattan in his chauffeur-
driven limousine. Occasionally they stopped
so that Ermine could take a photo for her
scrapbook.

Ermine felt quite awestruck by her new
surroundings. She had never seen such tall
buildings, or such beautiful shops, or so
many people hurrying along the sidewalks
wrapped up against the winter chill.

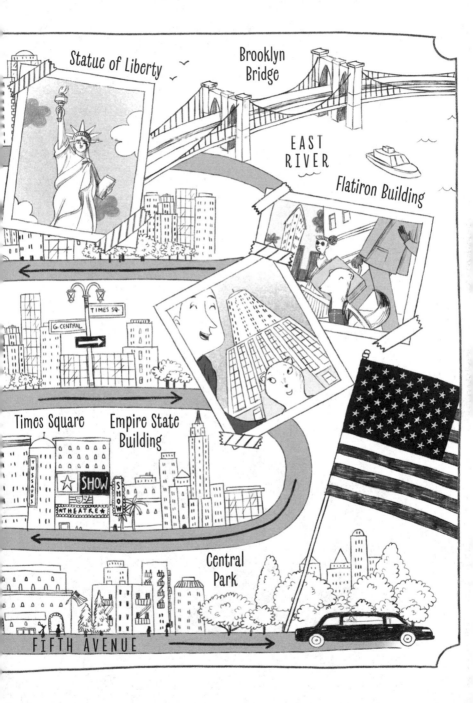

The shop windows were festooned with cut-out snowflakes, red ribbons and twinkling Christmas lights.

Bright yellow taxis honked their horns. Steam drifted from manhole covers into the crisp air.

Neon signs blazed.

Ermine rolled the window down and sniffed. There was a delicious sweet smell from the donut stands on the street corners. Her tummy began to rumble. She couldn't wait to taste American food!

She was quite surprised when, after a little while, they came to a big, green space.

"This is Central Park," Michael S. Megabucks told her.

The limo pulled up outside some wide gates.

"And this is the City Zoo."

"The zoo!" Ermine cried.

"Isn't that where you see all sorts of different animals from around the world?"

"Sure is!" Michael S. Megabucks grinned.

Ermine clapped her paws in excitement. "I've read about zoos. I've always wanted to go to one!"

"Well, now's your chance!" Michael S. Megabucks patted his overcoat pocket. Ermine wrapped her woolly scarf carefully around her neck, threw her camera over her shoulder, grabbed her tool bag and climbed into the pocket. The two of them got out of the car.

Just then a tall, dark-haired woman came hurrying towards them. She was wrapped up in an expensive-looking coat.

"Is that your ex-wife?" asked Ermine, with interest. The Duchess had told her the Megabucks were separated.

"Yeah, that's Susie – Mike's mom," Michael S. Megabucks replied.

Behind the woman trotted a small freckled boy, holding several large balloons.

"And that's Mike Junior!"

"Dad!" the boy shouted, running over and giving Mike Senior a hug.

Michael S. Megabucks ruffled the boy's hair. "Happy birthday, son!"

Susie addressed them both. "Now remember, no late nights, no soda, no junk food and not too much TV. And no getting into trouble." She gave Mike Junior a peck on the cheek and disappeared into a taxi.

"Can we go and see the animals now?" Ermine said from her position in Michael S. Megabucks's overcoat pocket.

Mike Junior noticed her for the first time. His jaw dropped. "What's with the talking weasel, Dad?"

"I'm not a weasel, I'm a stoat," Ermine said stiffly. "And my name's Ermine." Her whiskers twitched with annoyance. "Ermine's gonna be staying with us for a little while,"

Michael S. Megabucks said hastily. He didn't want the two of them getting off on the wrong foot. "She's come all the way from Balaclavia to see us. I thought you guys could hang out."

"Cool!" said Mike Junior, high-fiving Ermine's tiny paw. "Hi, Ermine!"

"Nice to meet you, Mike," said Ermine politely.

Michael S. Megabucks crossed his fingers behind his back. Mike Junior seemed quite taken with their visitor.

"Can I take Ermine to see the alligators?" Mike Junior said eagerly.

"I guess so." Michael S. Megabucks sighed, placing Ermine on Mike Junior's shoulder. "You two go on ahead. I'll buy us some popcorn."

The three of them went in through
the gates.

"This way!" Mike Junior pushed through
the crowd towards the alligator pen.

Ermine clung onto his shoulder. The zoo
was very busy. She didn't want to fall off and
get her tail trampled.

Very soon they arrived at some railings. On
the other side of the railings was a pit containing
a large pond ringed with bushes.

"There they are!" Mike Junior cried.

Ermine peered down. On the bank of the pond, three knobbly, brown alligators lay on the mud. "**Ooh, ooh, ooh!**" she squealed. She had only ever seen a picture of an alligator before. They were much bigger and scarier in real life than she had ever imagined.

"Hold these. I want to get a better look." Mike Junior thrust the strings of his balloons into Ermine's paw and poked his head through the railings.

Ermine suddenly felt herself being lifted into the air. She looked down. The ground was getting further away. The railings and Mike Junior were beneath her. Ermine felt a surge of panic. Flying was for birds, not stoats, and she didn't know how to get down.

"HELP!" she squeaked, but her voice was drowned out by the noise from the passing crowds.

Just then Michael S. Megabucks spotted the danger and shouted from the popcorn stall.

"HEY, MIKE! WATCH OUT! ERMINE'S FLOATING AWAY!"

Mike Junior looked up. "Don't worry, Dad. I'll get her." He made a leap for Ermine and missed.

"BE CAREFUL!" yelled Mike Senior. He started pushing his way through the crowds towards them.

"HELP!" screamed Ermine. Now the wind was sending her in the direction of the alligators. She waved her tail wildly back and forth to stop herself from drifting up, up and away altogether.

Mike Junior climbed onto the railings. "Wave your tail harder," he called to Ermine.

Ermine whizzed her tail round and round like a propeller. It seemed to be slowing her down.

"MIKE, GET DOWN!" Michael S. Megabucks yelled.

"I WILL ONCE I GET ERMINE!" Balancing shakily, Mike Junior reached out a hand and made a grab for Ermine.

He caught hold of her whizzing tail. "I'VE GOT HER, DAD!"

"EEK!" Ermine squeaked, just as a strong gust of wind caught the balloons.

"WHOOAAAAAAHHHHH!"

All of a sudden Mike
Junior found himself lifted
off the railings, rising a little
way above the alligator pen.

"LET GO!" he shouted.

Ermine let go of the balloons.

Now she felt herself
plummeting downwards at
an alarming rate, with
Mike Junior's fist still
attached to her tail.

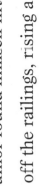

OOOOOHM,,

SNAP! CRA-ACK!

They both landed in the bushes.

The three alligators slid off the swampy bank into the pond and swam lazily through the water towards them.

Ermine glanced up. A crowd of onlookers had gathered to see the drama unfolding. They all looked very worried, especially a woman in a brown zoo uniform.

Michael S. Megabucks reached the railings. The woman spoke to him quickly, then sped off. "HOLD ON, GUYS!" he shouted. "THE ZOOKEEPER'S ON HER WAY."

"Tell her to hurry up!" Ermine squeaked. The alligators were even bigger and scarier close up. Their skin was scaly and wrinkly and they had powerful looking tails and long, flat snouts full of sharp teeth. They looked even more menacing than the foxes that used to chase her in Balaclavia when she was a kitten.

"D-d-do something, someone!" Mike Junior gulped.

The alligators were crawling towards the bushes on their thick, stumpy legs.

Ermine wondered what to do. She'd left her tool bag in Mike Senior's pocket. Then she had a brainwave. The thought of Balaclavia had given her an idea.

She wiggled up the front of Mike Junior's shirt. "Don't worry," she hissed. "I'll distract them." Quick as a flash she took off her scarf and gave it to Mike Junior along with her camera. "Hold these," she said. Then she turned and launched herself into the air, landing right in front of the alligators.

The three creatures looked at one another and grinned wickedly. They slithered forwards, jaws open.

All of a sudden Ermine
began to fling herself about.

She *tumbled*...

...and *flipped*.

She **somersaulted**...

...and *jumped*.

She **pirouetted** and **twirled**.

She looked just like an acrobat at a circus!

The alligators halted in their tracks.

They watched, entranced.

"What are you doing?" Mike Junior whispered.

"I'm dancing, of course!" Ermine puffed. "It hypnotizes them. We do it at home, only with foxes, not alligators. It stops them from trying to chase us."

Just then a metal door slid open at the back of the pen. The woman in the brown zoo uniform poked her head through.

"The zookeeper's here!" Mike whispered.

The zookeeper threw two lumps of meat to the alligators. In an instant, the animals came out of their trance and turned towards the snack, snapping at it with their great jaws.

"Quick!" the zookeeper called softly to Mike Junior and Ermine. "Over here! Run!"

Mike Junior raced out of the pen, closely followed by Ermine. She did a final backflip and with a whisk of her tail she was out.

CLANG!

The zookeeper banged the door shut behind them. "Whew!" she said. "That was close!"

Michael S. Megabucks was waiting in the concrete area behind the pen. He squatted down on his heels. "That was a terrible idea," he told Mike Junior. "I was worried sick."

"I know, Dad." Mike Junior hung his head. "I'm sorry. I sure won't do it again."

"And no more about alligators!" Mike Senior said.

"Okay." Mike Junior's freckled face broke into a grin. "Anyway, who needs alligators? I've got Ermine." He picked her up and put her on his shoulder.

Ermine squeaked in delight. She was glad Mike Junior wasn't in too much trouble. It was his birthday after all. And he hadn't meant to fall into the alligator pen. He was just trying to save her.

Michael S. Megabucks gave his son a hug. He straightened up. "There's some folks up there who want to meet you," he said to Ermine.

"Who?" Ermine said excitedly. She liked meeting new people.

"You'll see!" Mike Senior said.

The zookeeper led the way back up the steps and out onto the concourse.

The group of onlookers had swelled to a huge crowd. It now included several newspaper journalists and a TV crew who had been covering another story nearby and who had arrived just in time to film the whole rescue.

When they saw Ermine everyone broke into cheers. **"Ooh! Ooh! Ooh!"** Ermine squealed. They were all waiting to see *her*! She wished she'd worn her feathered hat.

"Can we get an interview?" the TV crew asked.

"Hang on a minute," Ermine said, waving at the crowd. She turned to the zookeeper and offered her a sweet smile. "Could I get your picture for my scrapbook?" she asked. "The Duchess did say I had to fill it up."

Chapter 4

On the other side of town...

Across the Hudson River in a run-down area of the Bronx, Harry Spudd was pacing the threadbare carpet of a dilapidated hotel room. The hotel was next to a railway line. Every so often a train clattered past, making the floor shake and the furniture rattle. It was a long way from the life of luxury the two brothers had been dreaming of for the last four years. In fact it was almost as bad as being in prison.

"The case must have gotten switched when the ticket fell off," Harry cursed.

"You mean someone else has our diamond?" Barry said. He was lying on his back on the thin mattress, counting the cracks in the ceiling. An unpleasant smell of boiled cabbage wafted from his dirty socks.

"They must have," Harry replied bitterly. "And we got their lousy hat."

"But why haven't they come forward to claim the reward?" Barry wondered. "I mean, it's like you said, Harry – if anyone had found the diamond, it wouldn't be a mystery any more." His face creased into an ugly frown. "Unless they stole it *themselves*."

Harry stopped pacing. "Maybe…" he said, unconvinced. The sort of person who deposited feathered hats at the Baggage Office didn't strike him as being the sort of

person who would pilfer a large diamond.
They were more likely to be the sort of
sickening do-gooder who would turn the
diamond over to the cops and claim the
reward.

And so far, it seemed that hadn't
happened. But even so, Barry had a point.
"Let's say someone *hasn't* stolen it," he said
thoughtfully. "Let's say they took it home
by mistake…"

"But why wouldn't they tell the police?"
Barry said.

"Because they don't know they've got it
yet!" Harry grabbed his brother by his shirt
and lifted him into the air so they were face
to face. "That passenger – the one with all
those little cases; the one who sent for her

66

luggage – what was her name?"

"I can't remember," Barry said. "Anyway, you said it didn't matter."

"Well, it does now. Her bags were about the same size as our case – I reckon the attendant must have mixed them up and sent the diamond on with all her luggage. We need to find her so we can switch it back before she opens the case." Harry gave him a shake.

"Stop it!" Barry protested. "I can't think straight if my brains are scrambled."

Harry held him still for a minute. "Anything?" he said, thrusting his chin at his brother.

"Um…Stott…no, Scott…no, Snot…no, Spot…no…" Barry started to cry. "It's no good, I can't remember."

Harry dropped him onto the bed. He pulled out his cell phone. "Never mind. I'll call up the Baggage Office and ask." He dialed a number. "Operator? Put me through to the Baggage Office. It's an emergency." He put the phone on loudspeaker.

BRRING BRRING! BRRING BRRING!

Hi, you've reached the Baggage Office. But guess what, we've all left for the day! Please call back tomorrow or leave a message after the tone.

BEEEEEP!

Harry threw the phone down in disgust.

"Aren't you going to leave a message?" Barry asked.

"Are you crazy?" Harry shouted. "And leave a clue for the cops?" He hurled himself onto the sofa and switched on the TV.

Barry was examining the dark blue case for clues of his own. He took out the feathered hat and tried it on. "It's very *small*," he said, regarding himself in the mirror, the tiny hat perched on his head.

"Maybe it's for a doll," Harry snapped, surfing through the channels. "Maybe she's

got a pet chihuahua. Maybe she just likes small hats. Who knows? It's too late now, anyway. We're never gonna find her."

He settled on the News Channel.

Barry slumped down next to him.

A broadcast was coming live from the City Zoo.

In breaking news, an amazing rescue took place here today when a small animal came to the aid of a boy who fell into the alligator pen. The animal, whose name is Ermine, hypnotized the alligators with a dazzling display of acrobatic dancing. Then she and the boy, who happens to be the son of one of New York's richest men – Michael S. Megabucks – raced to safety with the help of the zookeeper.

NEWS 24 BREAKING NEWS - an amazing rescue took place here.

"That's so cool!" said Barry. "I wonder what kind of animal did that?"

"I don't care!" growled Harry. He wracked his brains, trying to remember the conversation at the airport. **Stott, Scott, Spot, Snot** – Barry was right. It was definitely something like that.

A small white animal appeared on the screen. It had a long tail with a black tip, two coal-black eyes, white whiskers and a pink nose. It was wearing a blue pinafore dress and a woolly scarf.

"Awww, cute!" said Barry.

Harry ground his teeth. He hated animals. He hated rich people too, especially rich kids. He wished the alligators had eaten them both.

Tell us in your own words what happened, Ermine.
24NEW
Well, I just arrived in New York and it was Mike Junior's birthday, so we decided to go to the zoo. He likes alligators, you see. Or at least, he did before they tried to eat him. Anyway, he gave me his balloons to hold and I floated away and then when he tried to grab me we fell into the alligator pen. I saved him but really he was trying to save me...

"She can talk!" Barry said in wonder. "You gotta admit, Harry, that's pretty impressive for a weasel."

"I told you, I don't CARE!" Harry growled. All he could think about was the missing diamond. If everything had gone to plan, they'd have sold it to their old pal, Dodgy Don the diamond dealer, by now. And they'd be on their way to Hawaii with ten million dollars in the bank, not watching some ridiculous story about a talking weasel. If only they could remember the passenger's name! He scowled furiously at the white furry figure on the screen. "Anyway, it's not a weasel, it's a stoat," he said.

Barry blinked. The word "stoat" seemed familiar somehow. "Did Grandma Spudd keep those too?" he asked.

"Only around her neck," Harry said. "They make good fur collars, stoats."

"Oh," said Barry. The word rattled around his brain. Stoat. Stoat. STOAT. He'd heard it recently, he was sure.

> Tell us, Ermine, how did you manage to hypnotize the alligators?
>
> Oh, that! It's what I do with foxes back home. It stops them from trying to chase us. We're very clever like that, us stoats...

"See?" said Harry, interrupting the reporter. "What did I tell you? It's not a weasel, it's a stoat."

STOAT. Stoat. STOAT. Suddenly Barry let out a triumphant cry.

"Ohhhh YEAAAAAHHHH!!"

"What's up with you?" asked Harry.

"That was the name of the passenger – the one with all the bags."

"What was?"

"Stoat!" said Barry. "Not Stott or Scott or Snot or Spot. S.T.O.T.E. Stoat. I remember now."

Harry sat up. "Are you sure?"

"Yes, that was definitely her name – Miss E. Stoat."

Miss E. Stoat?! Harry looked hard at the screen. Ermine was waving at the cheering crowds. His eyes narrowed. "Hang on a minute, didn't she say she just arrived in New York?"

"What, you mean *that*'s her?" Barry gasped. "The one what took our diamond?"

"Shhhhhhh!" Harry leaned forwards and turned up the TV.

The Duchess?

Yes, she rescued me from the Duke when I was a baby. He wanted to use my fur to trim the collar of his robe. She lives in Balaclavia. She's the one who taught me how to use a wrench and when to wear a feathered hat...

The two villains stared at one another. Then they stared at the feathered hat. Then they stared at Ermine on the television.

"**IT <u>IS</u> HER!!!!**" Barry cried.

"Good work, bro!" Harry gave him a pat on the head. He rubbed his hands together gleefully. "Now all we've got to do is break into Michael S. Megabucks's apartment tonight and get our diamond back."

Chapter 5

Later that night...

Ermine tossed and turned. Try as she might, she couldn't sleep. She was in the guest room of Michael S. Megabucks's penthouse apartment on Fifth Avenue, overlooking Central Park. The enormous feather bed was the most comfortable she had ever been in, but the constant buzz of traffic from the street below and the excitement of the day meant she still felt wide awake. That, and the smell of the delicious leftover pizza that was sitting in the kitchen in a large cardboard box.

Ermine had never eaten pizza before tonight. Now she felt she could eat it forever. She had already made up some interesting toppings of her own, with the help of the chef from *Toni Balloni's*, the local pizzeria.

Cheese and cherries

Spicy beef and blueberries

Jalapenos and honey

Pumpkin and popcorn

Ermine's whiskers twitched at the thought. It was no good – the smell of the pizza seemed to be calling to her. She decided to sneak along to the kitchen and have a slice. She could do some work on her scrapbook at the same time!

She wiggled out of bed and pulled her bathrobe on over her pajamas. Then she tiptoed across the thick carpet to the closet where her bags lay in neat, colorful rows. Packed inside them was everything a world-traveling stoat could need. Blue was for hats, pink was for clothes, yellow was for undies and green was for coats. (Of course, Ermine didn't need shoes most of the time, because she had two perfectly good pairs of paws.)

She thought for a moment about unpacking – there hadn't been time so far, and she wanted to take her prized feathered hat out. But then she decided it could wait until morning. Her scrapbook was in the kitchen. All she really needed was glue and scissors. So she picked up her tool bag and crept out of the door.

Ermine pattered along the dimly lit hallway past the other bedrooms. Sounds of snoring – one loud, one soft – told her that the two Mikes were fast asleep.

ZZZZZZ ZZZZ... ZZZZZZZZ...

When she reached the hallway she paused. Propped up beside the front door was a brand-new skateboard. The skateboard was a birthday present for Mike Junior from his dad, but because of the adventure at the zoo he hadn't been able to try it out yet.

Ermine longed to try it out. Mike Junior had promised her a turn in the morning, but now she was up she didn't think she could wait until then. Besides which, if she practiced a bit *now*, then she'd be able to do it right when they went to the park tomorrow. She was sure Mike Junior wouldn't mind.

Ermine scurried over. She lowered the skateboard gently to the floor, hopped on and pushed herself off with her back paw.

WHOOSH!

Ermine felt the wind in her ears.
This was easy! And almost as much
fun as the sledding she did in the
winter back in Balaclavia!

Ermine glided to a
halt beside the kitchen, and picked up her
tool bag. The door was open a crack. Ermine
squeezed through. Carrying her tool bag in one
paw, she climbed up a stool onto the kitchen
counter and turned on the lights with
the remote control. Lying on the
counter beside the pizza were several
postcards of New York and a copy of the
Evening News, waiting to be cut out
and pasted into her scrapbook.

Ermine removed a hammer and
a box of nails from her tool bag so she
could reach the items underneath and laid
out everything she would need:

○	EXTRA-STICKY glue	☑
	Scissors	☑
	Stickers	☑
○	Pens	☑

She helped herself to a slice of cheese-and-
cherry pizza and set to work on the scrapbook.

Very soon she had created a lovely collage.

She finished it off with a few stickers. Then she sat back on the stool to admire her work.

SPLAT!
CRASH!

Ermine looked
around in alarm.
Oh dear! Somehow
she had managed to
knock the glue container
and the box of nails off the
worktop with her tail. She peered
down. On the floor a little way
away was a large puddle of
EXTRA-STICKY glue.
Beside it, nearer the
worktop, lay a forest of nails.

Ermine wasn't sure what to do. She didn't know where to find a mop or a broom, and she definitely didn't want to risk getting her tail stuck in the glue. It would be better to clean it up in the morning when the glue was dry. She hoped Mike Senior wouldn't mind. He probably got up early to go to work and he might not be very happy when he saw the mess in the kitchen…especially if the cleaning up made him late.

Suddenly Ermine had a brainwave. She would make Mike Senior breakfast to say sorry for the mess, and make sure he got to work on time.

She opened a cabinet to see what she could find.

Cola
Fizzymints
X-TRA STRONG chili sauce
Hot dogs
Buns

Ermine removed the items one by one and arranged them carefully on the counter. She stroked her whiskers thoughtfully. Normally she had boiled eggs and toast for breakfast, and she didn't really know what any of this strange American food was, but if it tasted as good as pizza, it would be just fine!

She arranged the hot dogs on a plate with the buns. After some hesitation, she decided the **X-TRA STRONG** chili sauce must be there to cool the hot dogs down.

Ftttssssszzzzzzz... Ftttszzzzzzz... Fttsszzzzzzzzzzzzzzzzzzz...

SPLOOSH! She poured it all over the top of the hot dogs in a big red splodge.

That left the cola and the Fizzymints.

Ermine considered for a moment. The Duchess liked to drink mint *tea* in the mornings. Maybe Mike Senior liked mint *cola*? She opened the bottle and dropped the Fizzymints in, one by one.

They gave off a pleasing hiss as they began to dissolve.

Suddenly Ermine let out a gigantic

YAWN.

She felt like she'd been
hit with a brick. It had to
be the jet lag catching up
with her at last. The
Duchess had warned her
it would.

Ermine screwed the cap
back on the cola bottle wearily.
Then she collected her tool bag,
turned off the lights, picked her way
carefully around the mess and headed
back out of the kitchen to bed. She was
fast asleep almost before her head touched
the pillow.

Chapter 6

The kitchen window of Michael Megabucks's mega-apartment flew open. Harry Spudd leaped nimbly through it. He was dressed in dark clothes and a balaclava, with the hat box tucked into his pocket. Barry's fat form squeezed painfully after him and collapsed beside the sink.

"Tell me again, why couldn't we take the elevator?" he groaned. The two brothers had climbed up the side of the huge apartment building using a rope and a grapple hook.

"Because someone might have seen us, you dope!" Harry hissed. "Now, come on."

Barry looked around fearfully. The kitchen was pitch-black apart from a thin finger of light coming from the doorway. "Can't we turn the lights on?" he whispered. "You know I'm afraid of the dark."

"No." Harry cuffed him on the head. "Use the flashlight."

Barry switched on his flashlight. A thin beam of light wobbled around the kitchen. It fell on the counter where Ermine had laid out breakfast.

"Food!" Barry breathed. He was starving.
The climb up the rope was more exercise than
he'd done in the last four years put together. He
tugged on Harry's sleeve. "Can I have some?
Before we start looking for the diamond?"

"No."

"Aw, please, Harry. Otherwise my tummy
might rumble and wake everyone up."

"Oh, all right then," Harry agreed.

Barry's tummy sounded somewhere between a volcano and an angry bear when it rumbled. It was a terrible trait Barry had inherited from Grandma Spudd. "Hurry up! And go easy on the cola – we don't want you burping."

Barry's burps were even worse than his rumbling tummy. It was another terrible trait he'd inherited from Grandma Spudd. (There was a third, but it's too rude to tell you about.)

"Okay." Barry tiptoed towards the counter. Suddenly he stopped dead.

"What's the matter?" Harry hissed.

"My feet are stuck."

"Don't be silly."

Barry pulled with all his might. "They are, Harry, honest." He held out his arms like a scarecrow.

Harry marched over. Then he stopped dead too. His shoes felt as though they'd been glued to the tiles. "What the...?"

"See?" Barry said.

"I told you."

"Take your shoes off. We'll step over it." Harry pulled one foot out of his shoe and took a giant stride forward. Then he pulled the other foot out of the other shoe and took a second giant stride forward. He beckoned to his brother. "It's fine over here."

"Okay." Barry made to follow. Unfortunately for him, his stride was much shorter than his brother's. Barry opened his mouth to scream.

"YEEEEOOOOOWWWWW!"

"Shut up!" Harry hissed sharply. "You'll wake up the whole apartment! What's the matter with you anyway?"

Barry's face went from red to purple. "I think I stepped on some tacks," he gasped.

Harry shone the flashlight on the floor. "You're right," he said. The area where Barry was standing was covered in nails. Behind that were two puddles of glue with two pairs of shoes stuck in the middle of them. Harry narrowed his eyes. "Someone's laid a trap," he muttered. He picked up Ermine's scrapbook and touched it gingerly with one finger. The glue was still wet. "Looks like it was the stoat," he said, examining the scrapbook.

"You think she's onto us?" Barry grunted.

"I don't see how she could be. Maybe it's

just a weird habit stoats have. Like guarding their territory or something. Now get over here."

Barry picked his way through the nails in his socks.

"OW, OOH, OW, OOH, OW, OOH!"

"Shhhhhhhhh!"

Barry reached the counter. "Hot dogs!" he said, rubbing his hands together in delight. "With ketchup! My favorite."

"Wait…" Harry began. There was something funny about the ketchup. It looked a little orange. "Maybe you should stick with the cold pizza."

But the first hot dog was already on its way into Barry's mouth. Barry bit down on the bun and chewed.

"YEEEEOOOOWWWWW!"

This time his face turned from red to purple to blue and back to red. He coughed and spluttered.

Harry slapped him hard on the back. "What's the matter now?"

"Hot...hot...hot...hot...hot..." Barry grabbed the bottle of cola and unscrewed the cap. Brown liquid spewed out. He raised the bottle to his burning lips.

"Wait..." Harry began again. The cola seemed awfully fizzy considering no one had shaken the bottle. And it smelled strongly of mints.

Barry ignored him. He took a long drink of cola. "Whew," he said, flapping at his mouth with his free hand. "That's better." He finished the bottle.

Harry picked up the discarded Fizzymint wrapper. He frowned. "Hey, Barry, remember when we were kids and Grandma Spudd used to make those cola bombs in the garden?"

"Yeah," Barry chuckled. Grandma Spudd's cola bombs were legendary. They had more power than your average jet-propelled rocket. "What about it?"

"What did she put in them to make the cola explode?"

"Fizzymints," said Barry. "Why?" He flashed the beam of his flashlight onto Harry's face. It wore a horrified look. "What's the matter?" asked Barry. Just then, he noticed a strange feeling in his gut. He looked down. His stomach was expanding at an alarming rate, as if someone was blowing it up with an air pump.

"I think I've got a burp coming," Barry said, his stomach churning. "You might want to cover your ears." He opened his mouth.

UUUUU
RRRRRRRRR
RRPPPPPP
PPPPPPPPPPPP!!"

The burp was so powerful it lifted
Barry off his feet. It was so gassy it set off
the smoke alarm.
BEEP-BEEP-BEEP-BEEP-BEEP!

The two villains heard the sound of a door opening down the hallway.

"Who's there?" a man's voice shouted.

"It's Megabucks!" Harry hissed. "Let's get out of here before he sees us. We'll take the elevator." He made for the kitchen door.

"Okay." Barry raced after him.

Harry rushed into the hall.

"**YEOW!**" He tripped over the skateboard and landed face down on top of it.

"**OOOOPPPPHHHHH!**" Barry toppled onto his brother, squashing him flat.

The skateboard surged forward. It shot across the hall and down the corridor past Mike Senior, who was coming the other way.

Mike Junior emerged from his bedroom.
"What's going on, Dad?
"We've got burglars!" Mike Senior
shouted. "They're making
a getaway. Look out!"
Mike Junior jumped out
of the way. The skateboard
was picking up speed.
Sparks flew from
its wheels as it
whizzed over
the shiny
floor.

"Make it stop!" shouted Barry.

Harry tried to use his toes to brake.

"I can't!" he screamed.

At the end of the corridor was a large picture window, which looked over Central Park. The skateboard hurtled towards it.

The two Mikes watched helplessly.

CRASH!

The glass shattered. The skateboard sailed out into the night sky, the Spudd brothers still on top of it. At that moment a noise erupted from Barry's bottom accompanied by an unpleasant smell. (I think you know what it was, but it's still too rude to mention.)

THHHFFFFFFFFFFFFFFFFTTTTTTTT

"Wow!" Mike Junior ran to the window holding his nose, and stared out. For a moment the two villains were silhouetted against the moon...

Then they disappeared from view.

From somewhere in the distance came a faint **splash**.

"Do you think they'll be all right, Dad?" Mike Junior said.

Mike Senior clapped a hand on his son's shoulder. "Yeah. As long as they can swim, that is. Sounds like they landed in Central Park Lake! Let's call the cops and tell them to pick 'em up." He steered his son towards the kitchen.

Mike Junior whistled. "I had no idea that skateboard was so fast, Dad."

"Neither did I." Mike Senior stopped abruptly. "Hang on a minute, what was it doing outside the kitchen anyway? I thought I put it by the front door."

The two Mikes looked at one another.

Ermine!

They started to laugh.

"Say, where *is* Ermine?" Mike Junior wondered.

"I'm here!" A small, white, furry face poked around the spare-room door wearing a cross expression. "I wish you'd stop making such a racket," Ermine complained. "I was trying to get some sleep!" She wrinkled her nose. "And what is that awful smell?"

Chapter 7

The next morning...

"All I did was try out the skateboard and make Mike Senior some breakfast," Ermine explained to the police officer.

They were in the kitchen at the apartment. The police officer (or "cop" as Mike Junior called her) was taking statements from everyone about the break-in, while another officer took photographs of the crime scene. A workman was busy boarding up the hole in the window at the end of the corridor.

"What about the shoes?" The police officer pointed to the two pairs of shoes glued to the floor.

"I knocked over the glue when I was filling up my scrapbook," Ermine told her. "It was the EXTRA-STICKY variety," she added. "I suppose they must have stepped in it."

"The EXTRA-STICKY variety…" The police officer wrote it down. Then she leaned over and sniffed the half-eaten hot dog. Her eyes watered from the heat of the chili sauce. "You made that?" she asked.

"Yes! I told you. It was for Mike Senior's breakfast. I wanted to make up for the mess."

Michael S. Megabucks raised an eyebrow. Even a drop of X-TRA STRONG chili sauce was enough to burn holes in the roof of your mouth, and it looked as if Ermine had used the whole bottle. He was glad the burglars had eaten it, not him.

"I used all the chili sauce to cool down the hot dogs," Ermine explained.

"That's not what it does," Mike Junior said. "Chili sauce makes food really, really spicy, especially if it's X-TRA STRONG!"

"Oh!" said Ermine. Honestly, there was so much to learn when you went on a world trip!

The police officer closed her notebook. "Well, Miss Ermine, I must say you sure set a good burglar trap!" She bent down, cut around the shoes with a pocketknife (avoiding the tacks) and levered them carefully off the floor. Then she placed the cola bottle and the Fizzymint wrapper into a plastic container for fingerprinting later. "What about this?" she said, holding it out to Ermine.

"It's mint cola," Ermine explained. "I put the Fizzymints in to give it some flavor."

"Mint cola?!" the police officer guffawed. "Are you kidding me?"

Ermine shook her head. "No, I promise. The Duchess drinks mint tea, you see, so I thought Mike Senior might like mint cola."

Mike Junior regarded Ermine with awe. "You made a *cola* bomb? *For real?*"

"A cola bomb?" Ermine looked horrified. "I don't know – did I?"

Michael S. Megabucks thought he'd better explain. "See, Ermine, if you add Fizzymints to cola, it creates a chemical reaction. After a while, it explodes."

"Oh," said Ermine. "Well I suppose I must have done that then."

Everyone collapsed in fits of laughter.

"Those burglars must have got one heck of a shock!" Mike Senior hooted.

"I wish I could have seen their faces when they realized what it was." Mike Junior chortled.

"No wonder they skateboarded out of the window!" the other officer roared.

Ermine felt her whiskers twitching. She could see the funny side now. She really *had* set a burglar trap, even if she hadn't meant to!

"We'll take these down to forensics for testing," the second officer said, his voice serious again, "but if you ask me, this is the work of the Spudd Brothers. Pity we didn't manage to pick 'em up last night but there was no sign of 'em when we got to the lake."

"The Spudd Brothers?" Mike Junior echoed. "You mean the diamond thieves? The ones who just escaped from prison?"

The officer nodded. "They fit the description you and your dad gave. One tall and thin; the other short and overweight."

"But why rob us?" Michael S. Megabucks asked.

The police officer shrugged. "I guess they just wanted to break into a nice apartment to see what they could find to tide them over."

"You mean you don't think they've gotten a hold of the missing diamond yet?" Mike Junior asked.

"I don't see how they could have," the police officer said. "Or, like your dad said, why would they rob you?"

"What missing diamond?" Ermine said, intrigued. This was turning into quite an adventure.

"A few years back the Spudd Brothers stole the world's biggest diamond from Toffany's, the famous jeweler's on

Fifth Avenue," the officer told her. "They were arrested and sent to prison for the robbery, but no one ever found out where they hid the diamond. Or at least, no one came forward with it to claim the reward."

"Reward?" Ermine squeaked. "What reward?"

"Whoever helps recover the diamond gets $10,000 and the opportunity to try on anything they want in the jewelry store."

"That sounds wonderful," sighed Ermine. She loved trying on jewelry – and she could put the photos in her scrapbook to show the Duchess! Plus $10,000 would go a long way towards mending the Duke and Duchess's leaky roof...

"Well, one small problem – *we* don't know

where the diamond is and the Spudd Brothers do," Mike Junior reminded them.

The police officer nodded. "You're right, I'm afraid. The thieves must be planning to pick up the diamond as soon as they can and make their getaway. It's our job to find them before they do. Anyway, we'd best be going." He raised his cap to Ermine. "It's been a pleasure meeting you, Miss."

"Can I have your photo for my scrapbook?"

Ermine asked. "The Duchess said I had to fill it up."

"Sure." The officer posed for a photo with Ermine. "And if you ever

want a job at the NYPD, give us a call."
The two officers let themselves out.

Michael S. Megabucks looked at his watch. "Shoot. I'd better go too – I'm late for a meeting. How about I meet ya later at the Rockefeller Center? You can show Ermine the sights. I'll send the limo to pick you up," he told Mike Junior.

"Okay, thanks, Dad."

Michael S. Megabucks threw on his coat and strode after the police officers.

"What's Rockefeller Center?" Ermine asked.

"It's where they have the huge Christmas tree," Mike explained. "It's got everything – shops, restaurants, a famous theater. It's even got an ice-skating rink…"

Ermine clapped her paws together in delight. "I love ice skating!" she cried. "And I've got the perfect outfit for it. It matches my white fur." She scampered off across the hall. "I'll go and get ready."

Back in her room, Ermine selected a pink suitcase from the closet and laid the contents on the bed, along with the other things she would need for her outing.

She quickly changed out of her pajamas into her skating outfit.

"Let's get the elevator to the Top of the Rock first and see the view," Mike Junior suggested from outside the door. "Dad's got VIP tickets. We can go anytime we like."

"Should I wear my feathered hat?" Ermine asked. The Top of the Rock sounded rather fancy. She retrieved the little dark-blue case from the closet and opened the catch.

"No," Mike Junior called back. "It's seventy floors up. It might get blown off."

Ermine snapped the catch back into place. She felt disappointed. She'd been looking forward to wearing her feathered hat. She rammed the skating boots into her tool bag, wrapped her woolly scarf around her neck and threw her camera over her shoulder.

Just then the intercom buzzed.

"The limo's here," Mike Junior shouted.

Ermine grabbed her tool bag. She eyed the dark-blue case longingly. She really *did* want to wear her feathered hat.

"Hurry up!"

She could always wear it when she went skating… Ermine picked up the little blue valise in the other paw and hurried out of the apartment after Mike Junior.

Chapter 8

Outside the apartment building...

Harry and Barry Spudd sat shivering inside their clunker car, keeping watch. They were both in a foul mood. The car heater didn't work right, they had no shoes, and their clothes were still damp from when they'd landed in Central Park Lake. They were also very tired and extremely hungry – without the diamond, they were broke.

"This is all your fault," Harry grumbled.

"I don't see how," Barry countered, removing a cheesy sock and examining his sore foot.

"You were the one who burped, remember?"

"Yeah, and you were the one who tripped

over the skateboard."

"Don't remind me," Harry glowered. He pressed his aching back against the car seat. He felt a lot *flatter* than the previous day since Barry landed on top of him.

"Anyway, now what?" Barry asked.

Harry patted his pocket, which contained the case with Ermine's feathered hat in it. "We'll wait until the kid and the stoat go out, then sneak into Megabucks's apartment and switch the cases."

"I'm not climbing up that rope again," Barry said, putting his sock back on.

"We'll find some other way," Harry said. He trained the binoculars on the apartment building.

Just then Ermine emerged jauntily through

the front doors. Clutched in one paw was a dark-blue leather case.

"Curses!" Harry spat. "She's got the diamond with her! We've got to catch her before she does anything with it."

Ermine and Mike Junior gave the doorman a wave and stepped into a sleek black limo.

Harry turned the ignition.

The engine coughed into life. The two villains pulled out after the limo.

"Don't lose them!" Barry said.

"Don't worry, I won't!" Harry replied.

BEEP! BEEP! BEEP!

The battered old car dodged through the traffic after the limo. They whizzed along Fifth Avenue past Toffany's. The sight of the dazzling diamonds in the windows made them more determined than ever.

After a little while, the limo drew to a halt outside the Rockefeller Center. Mike Junior emerged with Ermine sitting comfortably on his shoulder, the blue case in one paw.

"They're heading for the Top of the Rock," Barry said, clambering into the backseat to get a better look.

The best views
of New York

The car screeched to a stop. The Spudd brothers jumped out and slammed the doors. They hurried across the road and entered the building. Inside, crowds of people were milling around in the reception area, admiring a huge glass chandelier. Everything was decked out in twinkly lights and tinsel, ready for Christmas.

"Over there!"

At the other end of the reception area was the elevator hall. Ermine and Mike Junior were stepping into the one in the middle with an attendant.

Harry set off in pursuit, pulling his brother after him.

"Shouldn't we get a ticket?" Barry asked anxiously.

"We don't have time for that," Harry

snapped. "Hurry up or we'll lose them."

The two villains rushed forwards.

A uniformed elevator operator barred their way. He regarded them coldly. "Tickets, please."

"I told you we needed a ticket, Harry!" Barry said. He blinked, realizing what he'd said. "I mean, um, Harri-*et*!"

Harry turned red. "How much?" he snapped.

The elevator operator pointed to the elevator with Ermine in it. "Sixty-five dollars each for VIP, or thirty-two dollars each to join the line." He gestured to a long line of people that snaked backwards and forwards across the hall.

"That's highway robbery," Harry complained. He pulled a crumpled ten-dollar bill from his pocket. "That's all we've got."

"Then you'll have to take the stairs," the elevator operator said snootily.

1,215 stairs and quite some time later, the villains arrived at the observation deck.

Barry staggered out onto the platform and collapsed.

"Get up, you loser!" Harry said.

"I can't!" Barry moaned. Climbing the stairs to the Top of the Rock was more exercise than he'd done in his whole entire life! He didn't think he'd ever be able to walk again.

Harry gave him a weak kick. "Pull yourself together or you won't be going to Hawaii. Find the stoat."

"Okay, okay!" Barry rolled over and sat up. He pulled the binoculars from his pocket and searched the deck. Suddenly he let out a sob. Tears rolled down his cheeks.

"What's the matter with you now?"

Barry held out the binoculars and pointed mutely.

"For ferrets' sake!" Harry exclaimed, putting the binoculars to his eyes. Ermine and Mike Junior were getting back into the VIP elevator to go down! The little blue case was still swinging from Ermine's paw. Harry growled. His face set in a furious expression. "There's no way some stupid stoat's getting away with our diamond. Come with me." He grabbed his brother by the arm.

"Where are we going this time?" Barry groaned.

"To catch that elevator."

"But how?"

"You'll see."

They headed for a door. Attached to it was a large sign, which read:

DANGER
VIP ELEVATOR SHAFT
DO NOT ENTER

"You sure about this, Harry?" Barry said anxiously.

"Zip it." Harry unpicked the lock and pushed the door open. The two men slipped in.

"This way." Harry raced down the narrow passageway. "Hurry up!"

They rounded a corner.

The passageway ended in a narrow platform. Below that was a huge square void full of cables. And disappearing down it at considerable speed was the VIP elevator.

"We'll have to jump!" Harry cried.

"I c-c-c-c-c-can't," Barry stammered. "I'm scared of heights."

"Too bad." Harry gave his brother a shove and leaped after him.

"WHOOAOOAOOAOO

AOAAOOOOO!"

The two of them landed with a thud
on the top of the elevator. It rocked
slightly, then ground to a shuddering halt.

Chapter 9

Inside the VIP elevator...

"What's the matter?" asked Mike Junior.

"I'm not sure," the elevator attendant said, pressing the controls. He frowned. "It felt like something landed on the roof."

"Like what?" Mike Junior asked.

"Maybe it's a very large pigeon," Ermine suggested.

The elevator attendant shrugged. "Whatever it was it seems to have jammed the system. It's programmed to shut the whole thing down if anything happens." He sighed. "I guess we'll just have to wait for the engineer to fix it."

"No, we won't," Ermine contradicted him. "I can do it. That's why I carry my tool bag," she explained, "in case there's an emergency." She rummaged in the bag and selected a tiny screwdriver and a pair of pliers. Then she climbed up Mike Junior and perched on his shoulder. It was just the right height for her to reach the control panel.

"What are you going to do?" Mike Junior asked her.

"Override the system, of course," Ermine said impatiently. *Honestly,* she thought, *humans could be awfully slow!* She removed the metal faceplate with the screwdriver, her face a picture of concentration. "Here," she said, handing the faceplate to the attendant.

"Are you sure you know what you're doing, Miss?" the attendant asked anxiously. The wiring looked very complicated.

Ermine fixed him with a steely stare. "Of course I know what I'm doing – the Duchess taught me."

"Don't worry," Mike Junior told him. "Ermine can do pretty much anything if she puts her mind to it."

Ermine picked up the tiny pliers with her other paw. Very delicately, using the screwdriver and the pliers in her front paws, she rewired the controls.

"That should do it." She screwed the faceplate back on. "Try now."

The attendant pressed the button. This time it worked! The elevator shot towards the bottom.

"I told you she could do it!" Mike Junior grinned.

Ermine felt pleased. All the things the Duchess had taught her back in Balaclavia were proving to be very useful on her travels. Suddenly her sharp ears heard a noise. A high-pitched wailing seemed to be coming from somewhere above them.

"What was that?" she said.

"What was what?" asked Mike Junior.

"I thought I heard a scream."

The attendant shrugged. "Must have been

the wind," he said. "It whistles past when we go at full speed."

"What is full speed?" Ermine asked with interest.

The elevator's progress through the building was displayed on a screen. She hadn't really paid it much attention on the way up because she'd been so excited to see the view, but now she regarded it with intense curiosity.

"WHOAOO!"

They seemed to be hurtling down like lightning.

"365 yards per minute," said the elevator attendant. "It takes forty-two seconds to complete the ride."

"Cool!" Mike Junior said.

"No wonder it sounds like someone's screaming!"

"Yeah. It doesn't normally last this long though," the attendant said, as the noise continued.

"I'll get it checked out."

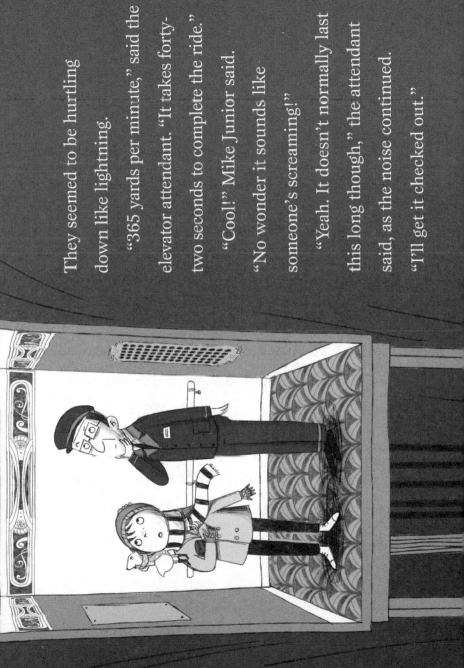

The elevator reached ground level. Ermine and Mike Junior waved goodbye to the attendant and made their way to the ice-skating rink.

"Ooh, ooh, ooh!" squealed Ermine. The rink was sunk into the middle of the Rockefeller Center, surrounded by glamorous shops and tall buildings. On one side was a beautiful golden statue rising out of a stone pond. Behind it was the tallest, bushiest Christmas tree Ermine had ever seen, even counting the forests back home in Balaclavia. It was dripping with thousands of different colored lights, which shone like enormous jewels. On the other side of the rink, steps led down to a viewing platform where lots of people were taking photographs. There was a lovely holiday atmosphere.

"I need to change into my skating boots,"

Ermine told Mike Junior. "And my feathered hat!" She was so glad she'd brought it.

"Okay, I'll get some milkshakes. What flavor do you want?"

"Pinenut?" Ermine suggested. She'd never had a milkshake before and wasn't sure what flavors were available.

"I don't think they have that," Mike Junior said. "How about strawberry?"

"All right." Ermine scuttled off to the locker room, clutching her two bags.

She removed her skates from the tool bag ready to put them on, threw off her scarf and rushed over to the mirror to check her outfit. The soft white velvet dress matched her winter fur perfectly. All she needed now was her feathered hat!

She reached for the blue case, flicked open the catch and lifted the lid. But instead of her feathered hat, her coal-black eyes fell on an enormous, glittering diamond. She picked it up and regarded it with astonishment.

Just then the door to the locker room flew open.

Two men stood framed in the doorway – one tall and thin and flat-looking, the other small and overweight. They both had very white faces and their hair stood straight up from their heads as if they'd seen a ghost. Neither of them was wearing shoes.

Ermine blinked at them. They looked

extremely cross,
although she couldn't
for the life of her think
why. Then she remembered
what the police officer had said
about the diamond and the two
thieves who had escaped from
prison. She gasped.

The Spudd Brothers!

"Looking for this, were you?"
Harry panted, opening
a small blue case.

Ermine regarded the
contents of the case
with amazement.

*Her feathered
hat!*

151

"Because we've been looking for *that*." Harry pointed at the diamond. "We hid it in the Baggage Office. The cases got switched at the airport."

So that was what happened!

"Only you wouldn't just let us switch them back when we broke into the apartment, would you?" Barry said menacingly. "You decided to give us the runaround."

"I didn't *mean* to," Ermine said indignantly. "It's not my fault you skateboarded out of the window into Central Park Lake."

"How about the chili dogs? And the cola bombs? And making us climb all the way to the Top of the Rock and risk our lives on the way back down again?" Harry hissed.

"Yeah, didn't you hear me screaming?" Barry put in. His hands trembled.

"I don't know how I wasn't sick."

"Oh, that was *you!*" Ermine said. It all made sense now. That was why the elevator stopped – the villains must have jumped on top of it. And the noise they'd heard inside the elevator really *was* someone screaming. No wonder the Spudd Brothers looked as if they'd seen a ghost!

Still, thought Ermine crossly, *it wasn't her fault – it was theirs!* The black tip of her tail twitched in annoyance. "You can't blame *me*," she said. "You shouldn't have stolen the diamond from Toffany's in the first place."

"Yeah, well we did. And now we're gonna take back what's ours…" said Harry.

"…and make *you* into a pair of earmuffs," Barry chortled.

Harry dropped the case containing the feathered hat and kicked it out of the way.

"Watch my hat!" Ermine squeaked.

"Forget your hat," said Harry.

"Yeah, and forget you!" added Barry.

The two villains advanced on Ermine.

"Hey, you clowns! Pick on someone your own size!"

It was Mike Junior! He stood in the doorway, clutching two giant strawberry milkshakes.

The villains rounded on him. "Get out of our way, kid!" Harry snarled.

"Or what?" Mike Junior held up the milkshakes. "Quick, Ermine, run!"

Still clutching the diamond in one paw,

Ermine slung her skates over one shoulder, dodged past the Spudd Brothers and scampered out of the locker room.

"Have these on me, losers!" Mike Junior cried. He hurled the milkshakes at the robbers.

SPLOOSH! The villains found themselves covered from head to toe with chilled pink milkshake. "She's getting away!" Harry spluttered, wiping a squashed strawberry from his eyes.

The two brothers pushed
past Mike Junior and set off
in pursuit of Ermine.
Ermine made for the ice
rink, the villains hard on her
heels. Quick as a flash she pulled
on her skating boots and shot out
onto the ice, the diamond in her paws.
The Spudd Brothers edged out
cautiously after her.
"Where'd she go?" Harry snarled.

"Search me! I can't see her anywhere."
Barry wheezed, clinging onto his brother.
Ermine had almost completely
   disappeared. Thanks to her white winter
   coat and matching skating outfit, she and
   the diamond were practically invisible
   against the sparkling ice.

Only one little bit of her gave her
away, and the villains were far too
preoccupied to notice what that was.
(I bet you can guess though.)

"I'm f-f-f-f-f-freezing!" Harry stuttered.

"M-m-m-me t-t-t-t-too!" Barry shivered, his lips blue.

"I c-c-c-can't move!"

"M-m-m-me n-n-n-n-neither!"

The combination of having no shoes, wearing damp clothes and being doused in strawberry milkshake was having an unfortunate effect on the Spudd Brothers. The ice rink was making them freeze from the socks up!

They ground to a halt in front of the magnificent Christmas tree, frozen solid.

"Yoo-hoo!" Ermine's voice floated up from the rink.

Mike Junior skated over. He looked hard at the ice.

SWISH, SWISH, SWISH.

A black furry arrow shot this way and that. Mike Junior grinned. It was the tip of Ermine's tail! He bent down and picked her up.

"Good work!" Ermine sat in Mike Junior's cupped hands, her skating boots dangling over his thumb.

"Here, this is yours." Mike Junior pulled her feathered hat out of his pocket.

"At last!" said Ermine, planting it firmly on her head.

Then she gave the villains a winning
smile. "You don't mind if I get a photo for
my scrapbook, do you?" she said. "The
Duchess did say I had to fill it up."

Dear Duchess,

I am having an amazing time in New York. I have made great friends with Michael S. Megabucks and Mike Junior (especially since I stopped him from being eaten by an alligator on his birthday). They've asked me to stay for Christmas! I have already been to lots of exciting places, like the Rockefeller Center, where I fixed the elevator and went ice skating. While we were there Mike Junior and I caught two robbers and recovered the missing Toffany diamond they stole before they went to prison. (The police had to come and defrost them before they were arrested, but that's another story.)

Today we're off to Toffany's to claim the reward. Mike Senior says you should have the $10,000 to fix your roof, which I think is a brilliant idea. And I get to try on all the jewelry I want! I am keeping my scrapbook up-to-date so I can show you all my photos when I get back. And don't worry - I'll make sure I get a really good one at Toffany's.

Merry Christmas!

Lots of love, Ermine

PS: Please could you write and tell me where I'm going next on my travels? I think I fancy somewhere hot.

Grand Duchess

Maria Von Schnitzel

The Imperial House of Hasbeen

Hasbeen Castle

Balaclavia

Europe

THE TRAVELS OF

Ermine

Sydney Superstar

How to make a travel

Ermine loves sticking photos, tickets, maps, postcards and more in her scrapbook as a way of remembering all the fabulous places she's visited. Why not give it a try yourself?

Step 1: Choose your scrapbook

Choosing the right scrapbook is very important. Think about how big you want it to be, what you might want on the cover, and what sort of paper you'd like.

Ermine's top tip: I love the smell of a new scrapbook, and I even chose a shiny ribbon to go around mine!

Sydney
AUSTRALIA

Er-mazing Ermine!

...oat set for stardom!

Step 2: Find your memories

Once you've found your scrapbook, it's time to start collecting. You can put anything in a travel scrapbook. Tickets? Check! Photos? Check! A leaf from a park you've visited? Check!

scrapbook like Ermine

Step 3: Stick it down

Now you're happy with the layout of your page, it's time to start sticking things down!

Ermine's top tip:

If I've used glue, I always leave my pages to dry out before closing my scrapbook.

Australia

Surfing stoat take: Sydney by storm.

SYDNEY

Step 4: Travel!

Decide where you want to travel to next...

Ermine's top tip:

I love to explore - from new countries and cities, to my own home, the outdoors, indoors and anywhere else I fancy. All you need is a dash of determination, a sprinkle of courage, and a dollop of curiosity!

Ermine's top tip:

I always place everything on the page first, so I can move things around and make sure I'm happy with how it looks!

Happy travels!

Dear Sylvia,

Thank you very much for offering to have Ermine to stay on her world travels. Since I adopted her she has turned out to be a very determined young lady with a great sense of adventure. I'm sure she and Butterfly will get along like a house on fire! Ermine also likes to help out, so if you need anything fixed she is definitely the one to ask. She will be arriving at half past eleven on Tuesday morning. I've told her to meet you at the Opera House.

With best wishes,

Maria Grand Duchess Maria Von Schnitzel

BALACLAVIA

OPEN LETTER

Dame Sylvia Lungstrom
C/o Sydney Opera House
Sydney
New South Wales
Australia

Chapter 1

At the Sydney Opera House...

Sylvia Lungstrom, the world's greatest opera singer, was feeling frazzled. There was only a week left before the curtain went up on her performance at the Sydney Opera House and she was late for rehearsal AGAIN.

The director would be upset. The cast would be upset. And Luciano Singalotti – who was playing the main part opposite her – would probably storm off stage in one of his famous tantrums.

Sylvia was never normally late. But having her eight-year-old granddaughter, Butterfly, to stay for the summer vacation made life much more complicated – especially as Butterfly thought opera sounded like a bunch of hyenas stuck in a garbage can.

Thank goodness she had called her old friend, Maria, for advice on what to do, thought Sylvia. And what a stroke of luck that Maria had suggested that Ermine should come and stay as part of her world travels. It would be a wonderful surprise for Butterfly to have a friend to play with, particularly one as unusual as Ermine! Sylvia smiled to herself. She could hardly wait to see the look on her granddaughter's face when their guest arrived.

But meanwhile she had a rehearsal to go to.

"Please hurry up, Butterfly!" Sylvia begged. The Opera House stood looking over the harbor. It was built on a great platform, like an ancient temple, and Sylvia and Butterfly had only reached the first level. There was still another big set of steps to go before they got to the stage door.

"I don't want to!" Butterfly dragged up the steps behind her grandmother. She was a slip of a girl with a gentle face and big, dark eyes. Right now though, she didn't look gentle at all. She looked positively ferocious. Her face wore a big scowl and her thick, cropped hair poked out in all directions from under a baseball cap, which she had on backwards.

The baseball cap was denim, like her overalls and sneakers. She was also wearing mismatched socks. "I want to climb the bridge."

Sydney Harbor Bridge was probably the city's best-known landmark apart from the Opera House. It formed a great arch over the harbor and Butterfly had set her heart on climbing all the way up to the top of it and all the way down the other side on the famous bridge climb.

"We'll do that later," Sylvia promised.

"But I want to do it now!" Butterfly sat down on the concrete.

"Butterfly…" Sylvia pleaded. "I'm late for rehearsal as it is. I need to practice."

"No, you don't," Butterfly said. "You just need to sing something decent, like Winifred Winnit does." Her face brightened. "Her performing wallabies are AWESOME!"

Winifred Winnit was a children's entertainer famous for songs such as "Kevin the Kangaroo" and "Kiss Me, Koala."

To Sylvia's trained ear, it was clear that Winifred Winnit could barely sing a note. But everyone in Australia, including Butterfly, absolutely adored her. Winifred and her wallabies had won the biggest talent show on Australian TV for two years in a row and were hotly anticipated to win this year's competition too, which was due to take place in just two days' time:

Sylvia had thought it would be fun to get tickets. But since she'd learned about

Ermine's visit, she'd had an even better idea…

Just then she heard a faint pattering behind her.

"Excuse me," said a voice. "I'm looking for Sylvia Lungstrom. Do you know where I can find her? It's just that this place is enormous and I don't know where to go!"

A brown, furry animal with a long, black-tipped bushy tail, two coal-black eyes, white whiskers and a pink nose stood beside Butterfly. The creature was about as high as Butterfly's knee and was wearing a blue pinafore dress and a straw hat.

A camera was slung over its shoulder and in one paw it carried a small bag marked TOOL BAG.

"Ermine!" Sylvia cried with relief. "You're early!"

"Sylvia!" Ermine squeaked. "It's you!" She removed a photograph from her pocket and examined it. "You look just like your picture, except without the horns."

"I only wear those onstage," Sylvia explained. She bent down and regarded Ermine closely. "And you look just like your picture too, except your fur is a different color."

"It's white in the winter," Ermine told her. "But in the summer it turns brown. We stoats are very clever like that."

"You certainly are!" Sylvia said. "By the way, this is my granddaughter, Butterfly."

Ermine held out a paw. "Hello," she said politely. "I'm Ermine." Then, "Did you fall or do you just like sitting on the ground?"

Butterfly gawped at her. "You can talk!" she said. She'd forgotten all about her tantrum.

"Yes, but I can't sing," Ermine said sadly. "At least not as well as your grandmother can." She clasped her paws together and looked up at the Opera House in awe. The roofs of the beautiful building towered above them like a set of billowing sails. "I can't wait to go to the opera and hear you sing, Sylvia," Ermine sighed. "I can wear my feathered hat!"

"Your what?" Butterfly said, getting up.

"My feathered hat," Ermine repeated. "The Duchess gave it to me. She adopted me when I was a kitten. She's taught me all sorts of useful things, like how to fix a bicycle chain and when to wear a feathered hat."

"Where *is* your feathered hat, Ermine?" Sylvia asked.

"With the rest of my luggage," Ermine said. "The taxi driver's bringing it. Look, there she is."

The taxi driver came towards them carrying a stack of small, brightly colored suitcases.

"You can put them in my dressing room," Sylvia told the taxi driver. She glanced at her watch. "Now I really must get going. Butterfly, you take Ermine to the cafe and get her something to eat…" She paused. "And while you're there, you can work on your act."

"What act?" Butterfly asked.

Sylvia's eyes twinkled. "The one you're going to do for *Australia's Most Awesome Animal Show*. I've entered you both in the talent competition."

"Really?" Butterfly gasped.

"Really." Sylvia smiled. "As long as Ermine agrees."

"Please, Ermine!" Butterfly begged. "I've always wanted to do something like that!"

Ermine didn't have to think about it for long. A talent show? It sounded exactly the sort of thing she'd be good at. She nodded. "Of course I will. The photographs will look amazing in my scrapbook! The Duchess said I have to fill it up so I have a record of my travels."

"Yesssssss!" Butterfly high-fived Ermine's paw and gave Sylvia a big hug. Then she bounded down the steps towards the harbor.

"Wait for me!" Ermine chased after her, the sun warming her fur. As she looked out over the blue water she had the feeling this was the start of a really big ADVENTURE!

Chapter 2

Beside the pool at Winifred Winnit's luxury house...

W inifred Winnit was lying on a sunbed under an umbrella, sipping a drink from a tall glass. Her face was covered in green mud and she had a piece of cucumber over each eye.

On the bed beside her reclined her pet Tasmanian devil – a creature about the size of a small dog, with dark fur, a broad muzzle and very sharp teeth. It had a gold collar around its neck and a pair of reflecting sunglasses perched on its nose.

"This is the life, Cruella!" Winifred said, removing the cucumber from her eyes and addressing her pet Tasmanian devil fondly. "Cheers!"

Cruella crushed the umbrella in her teeth and took a big **slurp** of her drink.

"Good, isn't it?" Winifred said.

Cruella burped.

Winifred looked around contentedly.
Winnit Mansion was her dream home. It
had everything a TV star could want: a pool,
a tennis court, a home theater, a popcorn
machine, seven bedrooms – one for each day
of the week – and gold toilet seats. It was the
kind of place you never had to leave because

everything was already there.

The only problem was that Winnit Mansion had cost a fortune to build and Winifred had no money left. Which was why she had to win *Australia's Most Awesome Animal Show* one more time. Then she could retire from showbiz and spend the rest of her life doing absolutely nothing.

"The prize money this year is a **MILLION DOLLARS**," she told Cruella. "We can just about manage on that. We could even get a Jacuzzi put in." Her face mask cracked into a sneer. "Better still, we can get rid of those loathsome wallabies *and* we'll never have to see another child again!" She cackled. "Horrible smelly things – and I don't just mean the wallabies."

Cruella growled her agreement.

"I suppose we should rehearse," Winifred groaned. "Although if I have to sing 'Kiss Me, Koala' one more time I think I'll be sick. I mean, who wrote that garbage?"

Cruella pointed a paw in Winifred's direction.

"Oh yes, you're right – it *was* me," Winifred remembered. "Which obviously means it isn't garbage, it's brilliant!" She sat up and reached for a towel. The talent show was going to take place in the big concert hall at the Opera House. Over two thousand people would be there, not to mention the fact that it would be televised live all over the country. It was the perfect opportunity to remind everyone how amazing she was. And she didn't want those stupid wallabies ruining it. "You'd better go and get the wallabies, Cruella," she said. "They need to practice their routine."

Cruella got down off the sun lounger and lumbered off in the direction of a dilapidated shed, which stood some way from the pool in a scruffy enclosure behind a high fence. The shed had several padlocks on the door to stop the wallabies from escaping. Cruella unpicked them one by one with her long toes and pushed the door open.

The wallabies shuffled out. They were similar to kangaroos, only smaller, with strong hind legs, broad feet and a long, thick tail, which made them excellent at hopping. They also had small front legs, which they used for play-boxing in the wild.

Cruella marched
the wallabies out of
the enclosure…

and down
some steps…

into a large basement
area of the house, where
Winifred had built
a rehearsal studio.

Winifred was waiting for them. She had changed into a colorful clown outfit. In place of the green mud, she had painted her face with freckles and warm rosy cheeks. Her blue eyes were framed with long fake lashes and on her head was a bright pink wig.

"All right, wallabies," she snapped. "Get into position or no dinner."

The wallabies formed a neat line behind her and linked tails.

Winifred pressed the remote.

The joyful sound of happy music filled the room as the wallabies began to sway back and forth. Winifred forced her face into a smile and began to sing in a baby voice:

"My mommy bought me a cuddly bear,
It sleeps upon my bed,
It's got gray fur and a fluffy tail,
And a square-shaped
sort of head.
Its nose is black and
its eyes are round,
And it lives in a
big gum tree,
Oh I love my koala
and I know my koala
loves me!"

Winifred's smile evaporated. She pressed
PAUSE.

"MORE ENERGY!" she screamed at the
wallabies. "DO SOME ACROBATICS!"

The wallabies bounced around. Two of
them got on unicycles. The others began to
form a wallaby pyramid.

Winifred pressed PLAY.

"So kiss me, koala, you know I love you so...
From your square-shaped head to your fluffy tail,
I don't want you to go.
Stay on my bed while I'm asleep,
We make a fabulous team..."

The smallest wallaby
took a run-up.

"If you kiss me, koala, I'll have a lovely dream!"

The wallaby landed perfectly on top of the pyramid on the tip of its tail.

Winifred gave the pretend audience a wink, rested her cheek on her hands in a gesture of sleep and closed her eyes.

The music stopped.

Winifred's eyes flew open again. "Not bad," she told the wallabies. "Now get lost."

The wallabies shuffled out with Cruella.

Winifred watched them go. She smiled to herself. She, Winifred, was as fabulous as ever, and there wasn't another animal in all of Australia who could beat her performing wallabies. The kids would go wild. There was no doubt about it: the prize money was in the bag.

Chapter 3

At the quayside in Sydney Harbor...

"I'm starving," Butterfly said to Ermine as they made their way to the cafe by the water. "Let's have brunch."

"What's brunch?" asked Ermine.

"It's a cross between breakfast and lunch," Butterfly explained. "Everyone has it in Australia."

Ermine thought for a minute. "Do they have lea as well?"

"What's lea?"

"A cross between lunch and tea."

Butterfly giggled. "No, silly, just brunch."
She led the way to a table at the waterside.

Ermine leaped onto the chair beside her
and admired the view.

Ferries ran back and forth, sailboats
bobbed on the sparkling blue water and

crowds of people walked along the wide
promenade. Behind them, the city's
skyscrapers rose up into the clear, blue sky.
Ermine thought she had never seen anything
so spectacular.

It was a world away from the snow-topped mountains of Balaclavia. It was also much hotter. Ermine was glad to have her straw hat.

The waiter came over. "What can I get you, Butterfly?"

"Corn fritters with syrup and bacon on the side for two, please," said Butterfly.

The waiter went to place their order.

"What exactly is a corn fritter?" asked Ermine curiously. The Duchess had told her it was good to try different types of food when you traveled.

"It's a sort of cake made out of corn," Butterfly told her. "Trust me – you'll love it!"

A cake made out of corn? *Now that was unusual,* thought Ermine. When she and the Duchess made cakes at the castle it was always a Victoria sponge cake.

Very soon the food arrived. Ermine helped herself. Butterfly was right: the corn fritters tasted delicious and the bacon and syrup gave them a sticky salty-sweet flavor.

"What do you eat in Balaclavia?" Butterfly asked her.

"I normally have eggs for breakfast," said Ermine, licking syrup off her whiskers,

"and rabbit stew for tea. I like fish too, especially if I catch it fresh from the river.

What about you?"

"I eat *tons* of fish," said Butterfly, "and rice and noodles. My dad's Vietnamese. He does most of the cooking when I'm at home." She beamed proudly. "And I get to help."

"How come you're *not* at home?" asked Ermine. "Are you on your world travels, like me?"

Butterfly giggled. "No, silly! It's summer vacation. Grandma offered to have me to stay. Anyway, how come *you* live with a duchess?"

"The Duke trapped me!" Ermine told her. "He wanted to use my fur to trim the collar of his robe!"

"But why?" Butterfly was shocked.

Ermine sighed. "It's very precious, my fur. It's called ermine, like me." She leaned forward to tell the story. "You see in the old days, when Balaclavia still had a king, the Duke and Duchess had to wear it around their necks when they went to visit His Majesty at the palace."

"That's horrible!" Butterfly said indignantly.

Ermine nodded sadly. "I know. The Duchess never liked it – she always said the only place for ermine is on a stoat. She didn't mind when the people got rid of the king. But the Duke was still very attached to his fur collar, which is why he caught me. Luckily the Duchess got back to the castle just in time to rescue me or I wouldn't be sitting here now."

"The Duchess sounds really nice," Butterfly said. "You should buy her a present from Australia to say thank you."

"That's a good idea!" said Ermine. "She needs a new hat. She spent all her savings on buying my around-the-world air ticket!"

Her face fell. "But I don't have any money."

"You will when we win the talent show!" Butterfly said. "Stay here. I'll go and get a pen and paper so we can write down some ideas for our act."

Butterfly disappeared inside the cafe.

As soon as she had gone, Ermine heard an incredible sound coming from somewhere nearby.

NYOW-WOW-WA-NYOW-WOW-WA-NYOW-WOW-WA

The sound reverberated up her tail and right through her body all the way to the tips of her whiskers. She found herself tapping her feet in time to the beat. Before she knew it, she had climbed down off her chair and run over to where the music was coming from on the quay.

She cast off her straw hat and started to dance.
NYOW-WOW-WA NYOW-WOW-WA NYOW-WOW-WA

Ermine *flipped*...

...and *somersaulted*.

She *cartwheeled*...

...and *jumped*.

She even did the **WORM**.
The music stopped.
She heard clapping. To
her surprise, a crowd had
gathered to watch her.

"That was pretty good," she heard a man say to her, as the rest of the people wandered away. "I've never seen a weasel dance to the didgeridoo before." "I'm NOT a weasel, I'm a stoat," Ermine bristled. "And we're very good at dancing – it's what we do in the wild." She looked up. The man had dark skin, black, curly hair that fell around his shoulders and a broad, kind face. In fact, he looked so kind that she decided to forgive him.

"True ay: you are very good!" He smiled. "I'm Eric."

"And I'm Ermine," said Ermine.

"And by the way, what *is* a didgeridoo?"

"This is." Eric patted a long wooden tube, which was propped up against his chair. The tube was about a yard and a half long, made from a textured wood and earthy in color. Ermine examined it carefully.

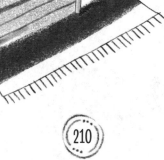

"The didgeridoo is one of the world's oldest musical instruments," Eric told her. "It's Aboriginal, like me. It makes the sound of nature – you know, the trees and the animals and the earth."

"It *does* remind me a bit of the forest in Balaclavia where I come from," Ermine said thoughtfully, "when the wind howls or the trees creak, or the animals call…"

Just then she heard Butterfly calling her name.

"That's Butterfly," Ermine said to Eric. "I'd better go. It was really great to meet you."

"It was great to meet you too," said Eric.

The two of them said goodbye.

Ermine went back to the table.

"There you are!" said Butterfly. "I wondered where you'd gone." She picked up the pen and paper. "Now, tell me what you're good at."

Ermine gave Butterfly a few examples. Butterfly wrote them down carefully.

☐ Climbing
☐ Fishing
☐ Swimming
☐ Sledding
☐ Fixing bicycles
☐ Solving diamond robberies

Butterfly looked at the list. "They're not acts!" she complained. "I meant singing or acrobatics, or something people normally do on talent shows!"

Ermine's eyes flashed. "Well," she said, a little stiffly, "climbing *is* acrobatic. At least, it is when *I* do it."

"I suppose…" said Butterfly.

"Maybe you're just not very good at it," Ermine suggested.

"Of course I am!" Butterfly responded. "I LOVE climbing."

"Trees?" asked Ermine, thinking of the pine forests in Balaclavia.

"No, bridges," Butterfly said.

"*Bridges?*" Ermine echoed, her curiosity aroused. She'd never heard of anyone climbing bridges before. "What bridges?"

"That one." Butterfly pointed to the

Sydney Harbor Bridge. "Grandma promised to take me this afternoon. You can come too! It'll be good practice if we do an acrobatic show. We need to get used to heights."

Ermine looked up at the enormous bridge. She could see a group of people making their way slowly along one of the metal arches towards the summit. They were so high up that they looked like ants.

She considered for a moment. "Can I get a photo at the top for my scrapbook?" she asked.

"Of course you can!" said Butterfly.

Ermine's whiskers twitched. She was never one to say no to a challenge. "All right," she agreed. "I'll do it."

Chapter 4

That afternoon on Sydney Harbor Bridge...

E rmine was perched on a narrow metal walkway high above the harbor. She was dressed in a blue boiler suit, with a headband to hold her ears back. The boiler suit had come from a doll in the souvenir shop, as there wasn't a suit small enough for her to borrow.

Luckily it fit perfectly!

Butterfly was at the front of the line, followed by Sylvia and Ermine. The rest of the group followed behind them, all wearing the same blue boiler suits with a rope clipped on

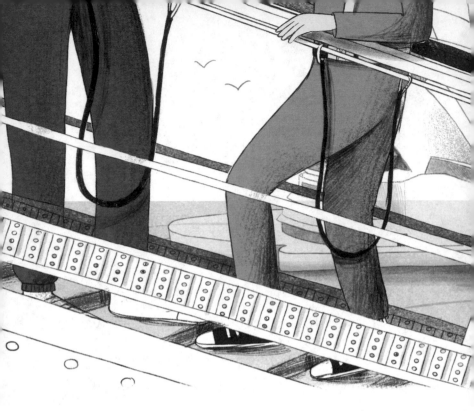

at the waist. The other end of each rope was attached to a safety rail so they couldn't fall off.

Ermine wished the Duchess could see her now. She felt very grown up and very brave! She peered down. The sea was a distant blue. They were already so high up that it was the

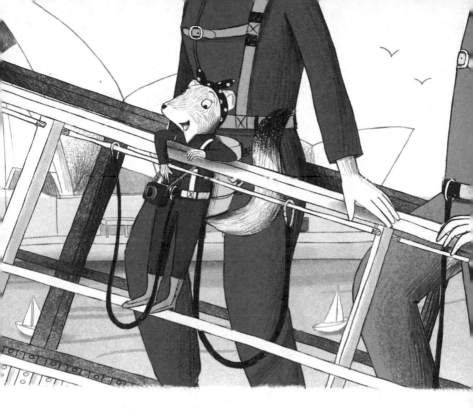

people on the quay below who looked like
ants now. And they had barely even started
the climb!

"Are you ready?" the guide asked.

"**READY!**" everyone shouted.

"Then let's go," said the guide.

Ermine leaped up the steps after Sylvia.

It was tough going for someone so small.

The higher they got, the windier it became.

"HELP!" she squeaked as the wind

battered her whiskers.

But nobody heard her –

the wind was too strong.

"HELP!" she cried again.

No one paid any attention.

wHOOSH!

Suddenly a great gust knocked her sideways. It blew her under the safety rail and off the bridge. Sylvia screamed at the top of her mighty opera-singer's voice. The sound was deafening. Even the wind seemed to stop for a few seconds.

Ermine dangled helplessly beneath the metal steps on the end of the rope.

"HOLD ON, ERMINE!" cried Butterfly.

"I'LL HELP." She crouched down and reached under the safety rail to grab the rope, ready to pull Ermine up.

"WAIT!" shouted the guide.

But it was too late.

WHOOOOSH!

There was an even stronger gust of wind.

Sylvia screamed again, even louder.

This time it was Butterfly who got knocked under the safety rail and off the bridge! She dangled beside Ermine.

The guide leaned over the rail while the rest of the group huddled together in fright.

"DON'T WORRY," she shouted. "WE'LL HAVE YOU SAFE AND SOUND IN NO TIME. JUST HANG ON WHILE I CALL FOR BACK-UP."

She got out her walkie-talkie.

But Butterfly wasn't worried.

"Hey, Ermine," she said, "we could do a trapeze act in the talent show. Check this out!" She began swinging backwards and forwards on the rope with all her might.

"*Wheeeeee!*" she cried, zipping back and forth.

"Wheeeeeeeeeeeeeeeee! Wheeeeeeeeeeeeeeeee eeeeeeeeeeeee!"

Just then there was a ripping sound.

Ermine gasped. Where the rope clipped onto Butterfly's boiler suit, the cloth had begun to tear. "Butterfly!" she squeaked. "Your suit's ripping. Stay still!"

Butterfly froze. But she couldn't stop the rope from swinging, or the boiler suit from tearing.

RRRRIP!

The tear in the cloth was getting bigger.

Sylvia's anxious face appeared above them, surrounded by the other members of the group. "DO SOMETHING, ERMINE!" she pleaded. "BUTTERFLY MIGHT FALL!"

Ermine glanced at the dizzying drop beneath them. She had to act fast. Suddenly she remembered her tool bag. Her face took on a determined expression. She knew exactly what to do. "DON'T WORRY, SYLVIA," she called back. "I'LL SAVE HER!"

The next time Butterfly swung by, Ermine reached out with her front paws and made a grab for the girl's foot…

SNATCH!

The two of them swung backwards and forwards together on the end of their ropes. It really *was* like a trapeze act, thought Ermine, who had once been to the circus with the Duchess. Only there was no safety net. She had to hurry.

She wiggled her way up Butterfly's leg…

SQUIRM!

And into her pocket…

PLOP!

From there she pulled the tool bag out of
her own boiler suit, opened it carefully and
felt inside.

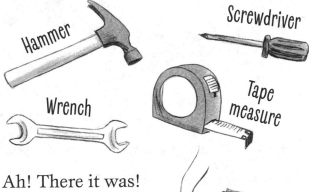

Hammer

Screwdriver

Wrench

Tape
measure

Ah! There it was!

Needle and thread.

Quick as a flash, Ermine threaded the needle.
She bit the thread with her sharp teeth and tied
a knot in the end. Then she began to sew.

Stitch! Stitch! Stitch!
Stitch! Stitch!

Up and down flew her paw…

Up and down and in and out…

In tiny, neat stitches…

Until the tear in

Butterfly's boiler suit was

completely mended.

"Hooray!" sang Sylvia. "Ermine's done it! She's saved Butterfly! She really *is* Australia's most awesome animal!"

"HOORAY!" shouted the group. Everyone up on the bridge hugged one another in delight.

"Where did you learn to do that?" Butterfly asked Ermine in amazement.

"The Duchess taught me, of course!" said Ermine, ducking back down into Butterfly's pocket to get out of the wind. It was bending her whiskers!

Just then they felt a pull on the rope. A team of guides had arrived. Very soon they were hauled to safety on the bridge. The group of climbers clapped and cheered.

"Oh, Butterfly! Thank goodness you're

230

safe!" Sylvia enveloped her granddaughter in her arms. For once, Butterfly didn't complain. She hugged Sylvia as hard as she could.

"Watch out for me!" said a small voice.

Sylvia stepped back.

Ermine poked her head out of Butterfly's pocket, looking a little squashed.

"Maybe we won't do acrobatics in the show after all," Butterfly said.

"I think that's a very good idea," agreed Sylvia.

"So do I," said Ermine. "I really don't think Butterfly's good enough at climbing yet." She straightened her whiskers. "Could someone please take a photograph?" she asked the group. "I'd like to put it in my scrapbook to show the Duchess."

Chapter 5

Later that evening at Winnit Mansion...

Winifred Winnit was standing in front of a mirror practicing her acceptance speech for winning *Australia's Most Awesome Animal Show*, when her computer began to ping.

PING
PING
PING
PING
PING

Winifred frowned. That meant people were talking about the competition on social media.

And they weren't just talking about it – they were going nuts!

Curses! she thought. One of her rivals must have posted something. She wondered which one it could be.

Paul Piggott and
Pete the percussion-
playing platypus?

Lucy Sponge
and Sue the
sighing sloth?

Bill Trogg and
Bert the bearded
tarantula?

Probably Bill Trogg, Winifred decided. Posting some pathetic piffle about his awful arachnid was just the sort of dirty, low-life trick that big-headed boaster would use to get publicity. She snorted. As if Bill Trogg and his tarantula could beat Winifred Winnit and her performing wallabies to a million dollar prize! The idea was ridiculous. All that spider did was crawl around.

Winifred reached for the computer and scrolled through the posts. Her face went pale.

It wasn't Bill Trogg and his bearded tarantula everyone was going crazy about.

The internet was abuzz with stories about some revolting child named Butterfly and – Winifred could hardly believe it – Ermine, a sewing *stoat*.

○ ○ ○ ◉

🌐 **AUSTRALIA NEWS**

NEW

DARING STOAT IS NEW DARLING OF SYDNEY!
Is Ermine Australia's Most Awesome Animal?

Winifred almost fainted.

AUSTRALIA NEWS Finance

**Sydney today witnessed one of the most
extraordinary events in its entire history when
Ermine, a brave young stoat, came to the rescue
of Butterfly Lungstrom, the granddaughter of
our very own opera star, Dame Sylvia.**

The three of them were taking
part in Sydney's famous bridge
climb experience when Ermine
and then Butterfly were blown
off the bridge by high winds.

She forced herself to read on.

When the stitching around Butterfly's safety clip began to tear, Ermine saved her life in a dazzling display of speed darning.

Butterfly (8) has confirmed that they will be entering Australia's Most Awesome Animal Show but they haven't yet decided on their act.

Ermine was not available for comment but, judging by the incredible response to Ermine's exploits, she and Butterfly must already be hot favorites to win. Last year's winners – Winifred Winnit and her performing wallabies – had better watch out!

Winifred Winnit ground her teeth. *Not available for comment!* What a stupid thing to say! Of course the stoat wasn't available for comment – that was because it couldn't speak! A stoat was just another dumb animal, like all the rest of them, even if it *could* sew.

She clicked angrily on a video link. One of the other climbers in the group had filmed the whole episode.

Butterfly and Ermine dangled from the bridge. *"DO SOMETHING, ERMINE!"* came a voice – Sylvia Lungstrom's, thought Winifred, judging by the volume. She saw the stoat's face take on a determined expression.

"DON'T WORRY, SYLVIA, I'LL SAVE HER!" it said.

IT COULD TALK??!!!!!!!!! Winifred's jaw dropped. Her eyes popped. She sat through the rest of the video in a daze.

Just then Cruella pottered in, looking for food. When she saw Ermine on the computer screen, she growled. Then she picked up a cushion in her gigantic teeth and shook it until all the feathers came out.

Winifred snapped out of her trance. She jumped to her feet and kicked the feathers in the air. "Silly, sewing stoat! Thinks it can steal my prize, does it? We'll see about that! I'll...I'll..."

Winifred paused for a moment.

What would she do?

Then she had an idea. A sewing stoat would come in very handy around the house, especially one that had a tail like a duster. She would find it, catch it and make it work for its keep.

"Quick, Cruella!" she snapped. "Get the costume box. We'll need a disguise if we're going to catch it."

Winifred had a very large collection of costumes, mainly thanks to all the children's parties she had entertained at before she became famous. Cruella dragged over a large trunk they were kept in and threw open the lid with her snout. Then she leaped into it and started to hurl its contents all over the room.

Winifred picked up a few things to examine them before tossing them aside impatiently.

Dorothy
and Toto

Goldilocks
and the one bear

Kangaroo
and joey

Little Red Riding Hood
and the wolf

*Little Bo Peep
and a sheep*

"No! No! No!"

Winifred cried. "That
Butterfly girl looks far too
smart to fall for any of those.
She mustn't suspect anything. We
need to blend in with the crowd."

Cruella burrowed deeper.
Costumes littered the room.

"Wait!" Winifred said.
She picked one up off the floor.

Surfer dude and dog...

"This is perfect, Cruella!" Winifred cried. She tried on the wig and glasses and admired herself in the mirror. She looked so dude-like, even her number one fan wouldn't recognize her. She gave an evil chuckle. All they had to do now was follow Butterfly and Ermine, wait until the child's back was turned, then nab the stoat and

keep it hard at work until the talent show was over and they were winners – by which time Winnit Mansion would be spotlessly clean as well.

Winifred was so happy she felt a new song coming on.

Easy, peasy. Ermine squeezy!
Catch the stoat and make it squeegee,
Use its tail to dust down low,
While Winifred wins the talent show!

There was just one thing she needed to do. Winifred picked up the phone and dialed the number of her agent.

"Gustav? Is that you? Now listen carefully. I need some information. I want you to find out where Sylvia Lungstrom lives…"

Chapter 6

The next morning at Sylvia's house...

Ermine and Butterfly were having breakfast in the garden. The house was a twenty-minute ferry ride from Sydney Harbor, perched on a hill overlooking the ocean. Beneath them lay a pretty, sheltered cove full of crystal-clear water where a few sailboats were moored. Ermine would have liked to go and explore. But that would have to wait: the show was tomorrow and they still didn't have an act.

Butterfly was looking through Ermine's list of talents. She had already crossed out *climbing*.

The next one of Ermine's talents was fishing.

"That's not a bad idea," Butterfly mused. "We could get a giant tank of fish and see how many you can catch. I could cook them," she added excitedly. "I *love* cooking! That could be my talent! We can work together."

"All right," said Ermine, popping a delicious piece of mango into her mouth and chewing it with relish. "But I might need a little practice. I haven't been fishing since I started my world travels."

Butterfly beamed. "I know just the place," she said. "I'll ask Grandma if she can drop us off on her way to rehearsal."

A little while later Ermine sat on the top deck of a ferry with Sylvia and Butterfly, shielded by her straw hat. She was taking snapshots with her camera to paste into her scrapbook. The ferry took them past all sorts of interesting places. She hoped she'd be able to visit them after the talent show.

Botanic
Gardens

National Maritime Museum

Luna Park

Sydney Opera House

Taronga Zoo

She even took
a selfie of herself
and Butterfly!
"Here we are!"
said Butterfly.

The three of them got off the boat. A surfer dude with big hair and a bandana got off too. He was with a small, black, muscly dog with a long tail. Both of them were wearing shades.

Ermine stared at them. "What's that for?" she whispered. She pointed at the board the surfer dude was carrying.

"It's a surfboard, silly," Butterfly whispered back. "You know, for riding waves."

Ermine didn't know, but it sounded fun anyway – she imagined it was a little like sledding, but on water instead of snow.

"I'll show you how to do it later when we go to the beach," Butterfly promised. They got into the ticket line for the aquarium. So did the surfer dude and his dog. Sylvia bought them tickets. "I'll send Derek, my housekeeper, to pick you up," she promised. "Then this evening I want to hear all about your act and see the dress rehearsal. You need to be prepared for tomorrow!" She waved goodbye and got back on the ferry to the Opera House. The sound of Sylvia practicing her scales washed around the bay.

Ermine and Butterfly went into the
aquarium, followed by the surfer
dude and his dog.

Ermine gazed at the huge
fish tanks with astonishment.
She had never seen so many
species of fish, or realized that
they could come in so many
shapes and sizes and colors.

"What are those?" she asked,
pointing to a tank full of pale,
floating balloon-like
creatures.

"They look easy to catch."

"Don't be silly," said Butterfly.

"They're jellyfish – they'll sting you."

"What about these?" The next tank contained flat triangular fish with long tails.

"Definitely not," said Butterfly. "They're stingrays. They'll sting you even worse."

They went into a tunnel. Ermine's eyes widened. It was like being underneath the sea! Above her, schools of silver fish swished this way and that.

"I could catch those," she suggested, pointing at the silver fish.

Butterfly snorted. "Sure! If you want to get eaten by a shark!"

A huge, snarling gray fish with beady, black eyes and a jagged fin swam towards them.

Ermine jumped back. "No, thank you!"
she said.

The tunnel ended. Butterfly dashed
forwards towards the next section. "Come on,
Ermine!" she said. "It's the rock pool!"

"Rock pool?" Ermine queried, scurrying
after her.

"You know," said Butterfly, "it's the fun
part where we're allowed to touch the fish."
She dashed up to the attendant. "Excuse me,"
she said politely, "would it be all right if
Ermine practiced her fishing? It's for
Australia's Most Awesome Animal Show –
we're trying to work out our act."

The attendant grinned. He recognized
Butterfly and Ermine from the rescue on
the bridge. "No worries," he said to Ermine.

"As long as you promise to be careful and put everything back and not hurt it."

"I promise!" Ermine said solemnly.

Ermine climbed up to the edge of the rock pool and looked down. As well as lots of little fish, there were all sorts of other interesting things she'd only ever seen in the Duchess's encyclopedia before.

Turtle

Sea urchins

Crab

Lobster

Sea Cucumber

Squid

Starfish

Ermine leaned over. She fished about in the rock pool with her paw and gently pulled out a squid.

"Good catch!" said Butterfly.

Ermine wasn't so sure. The squid didn't look very pleased to be disturbed.

"LOOK OUT!" shouted the attendant.

A great cloud of ink squirted from the squid.

Ermine ducked just in time. She didn't want her fur to get dirty!

"YEEEEOOOOWWWWW!"

Ermine looked up. It was the surfer dude! He had propped his surfboard against the wall and was standing right next to her with his dog. He had taken off his sunglasses, and his eyes were now dripping with black squid ink! *What a silly place to stand,* thought Ermine.

She carefully returned the angry squid to the water.

"Try a crab," suggested the attendant.

"Okay."

Ermine pounced on a crab. Only she was so shocked when she held it up and saw its two eyes staring back at her on stalks, she accidentally dropped it.

The crab landed on the surfer dude's dog. It nipped its nose as hard as it could.

"RRRAAOOOWW!"

squealed the dog.

The dog too! thought Ermine. *You'd think it would move when it saw what happened to its owner.*

She picked the crab up carefully and put it back in the pool.

"Have another try," said the attendant.

This time Ermine went for the sea cucumber. Only it was so slippery that it shot straight out of her paws and

landed on the surfer dude's forehead.

SPLAT!

The surfer dude stood rooted to the spot. The sea cucumber slid slowly down his cheek before dropping back in the pool and drifting calmly away to safety.

Some people just don't learn! Ermine thought.

The surfer dude's face was streaked black from the squid ink and was covered in slime. He looked as if he was dressed up for a Halloween party. Ermine felt the urge to giggle.

The attendant stepped forward with a packet of wet wipes. "No worries, mate. We'll have that off in a jiffy," he said. He began dabbing at the surfer dude's face.

To Ermine's surprise, the surfer dude pushed the attendant roughly away.

"*Get off me!*" he hissed, taking a giant step backwards – which was when he tripped over the dog and fell over the barrier into the rock pool.

"OOOWOWWWWWWWW!"

he howled.

"Oh dear," Butterfly said, "I think he sat on a sea urchin."

"I hope it's all right," Ermine said in a worried voice, peering into the rock pool.

"It will be," the attendant reassured her.

The surfer dude plucked the sea urchin from his tattered wetsuit and placed it back in the pool. He climbed awkwardly over the barrier, collected his surfboard and limped painfully past Ermine and Butterfly towards the exit, leaving a trail of drips in his wake.

Underneath the wet suit the surfer dude

was wearing a pair of bright pink, frilly underwear.

Ermine thought they looked most unsuitable for surfing.

"Do you want to help me feed the sharks?" the attendant asked hopefully. Butterfly shook her head. "We'd better go," she said.

"Thanks for letting me practice," said Ermine.

"No worries," said the attendant. "Good luck with the competition! I hope you win!"

Ermine and Butterfly made their way to the exit to meet Derek.

"Maybe fishing's not such a good idea after all," Ermine sighed.

"I agree," said Butterfly. "But what are we going to do instead?"

"Let's go to the beach," Ermine suggested. Her black eyes sparkled with excitement. "We can think about it more there, while you're teaching me to surf."

Chapter 7

That afternoon at the beach...

Winifred Winnit sat on the beach, keeping watch through a pair of binoculars. She was still wearing the remains of the surfer dude outfit. Her wetsuit was full of holes where the sea urchin had spiked it, her eyes stung from the squid ink and her skin felt slimy.

Cruella lay beside Winifred, nursing her sore nose.

Butterfly was teaching Ermine how to surf. The two of them were getting used to their boards in the shallows, away from the strong waves further out to sea.

The problem for Winifred was that there were lots of other people around. The spot Ermine and Butterfly had chosen was right in front of the lifeguards' enclosure, where it was safe to swim. And there was a grown-up nearby, keeping an eye on them.

"*Curses!*" Winifred zoomed in with the binoculars. "We have to catch that senseless stoat!" The arrogance of the animal was breathtaking. How dare it do all those awful things to her at the aquarium and not even apologize? And then for the stoat just to head to the beach and start swimming without a care in the world. Winifred gnashed her teeth. She was more determined to win the talent show than ever. She had to have that Jacuzzi. She just had to!

Suddenly, an announcement came over the loud speaker.

"WOULD ALL THE COMPETITORS IN TODAY'S JUNIOR SUPER SURFER COMPETITION PLEASE MAKE THEIR WAY TO THE LIFEGUARD ENCLOSURE IMMEDIATELY."

Ermine and Butterfly got out of the water with the other kids and lined up in front of the lifeguard tent.

Easy, peasy, Ermine squeezy...

Winifred's eyes gleamed. An idea began to form in her mind. If Ermine was entering the contest, she would be out there on the water surfing all alone. This was their opportunity to grab her. *But how?* She, Winifred, couldn't very well enter a kids' surfing competition. It would attract too much attention. And even though she looked the part (apart from the frilly underwear), she wasn't a very strong swimmer…

Just then, Winifred spied another tent further down the beach.

Paddle Boats for Rent

"Come on, Cruella." Winifred sprinted along the beach to the paddle boat tent. It was closed. There was a line of blue paddle boats chained up outside. "Quick, Cruella!" she hissed.

Cruella opened her jaws wide and bit straight through the chain with her enormous teeth.

"Good work!" Winifred pulled one of the paddle boats free. Then she hauled it along the sand to the water's edge and jumped in.

Cruella jumped in after her.

The two of them pedaled furiously through the surf.

SPLASH! SPLASH! SPLASH! SPLASH!

Out on the water, the Junior Super Surfer Competition was in full swing. The kids had paddled out to sea on their surfboards and were shooting this way and that on the breaking waves. But to Winifred's confusion, Ermine and Butterfly were not among them. Now what were they doing?

Winifred raked the sea with her binoculars. "There they are!" she said.

Ermine and Butterfly had paddled further out. They seemed to be waiting for something.

"Step on the gas, Cruella!" Winifred steered the paddle boat towards them, her thighs burning from the exercise. All of a sudden, the pain in her legs eased. The tide was sucking the paddle boat out to sea, away from the beach. Very soon, Winifred and Cruella drew level with their targets.

Ha ha! thought Winifred. This was going to be easier than she'd imagined. Butterfly and Ermine hadn't even noticed their approach. Butterfly was too busy pointing at something on the horizon.

To Winifred's surprise, Cruella began to whimper. "What's wrong with you?" she snapped.

Cruella pointed a paw in the same direction as Butterfly. Winifred turned around to have a look. She blinked.

An enormous wave was forming.

Winifred felt the paddle boat
being lifted up. The sea became a
hill, then a mountain. The water
fell away beneath them in a vertical
slope. The paddle boat teetered on
the crest of the huge wave.

Winifred's mouth formed a
very large 0.

Cruella gave a terrified yelp.

"WOOHOOO!"

"WOOHOO!"

Just then Butterfly whizzed past
them on her surfboard. So did Ermine.

The two of them hurtled down the
mountain of water like skiers in a race
– Butterfly ahead by a whisker.

"WHOOOOOAAAAA

The paddle boat plunged after them, lurching from side to side. Winifred and Cruella clung on for dear life.

Above them the wall of water began to curve. Very soon, the wave curled into a tunnel.

Butterfly and Ermine zipped along it, neck and neck.

The paddle boat careered after them.

Winifred and Cruella bounced off the edges of the tunnel of water.

They neared the shore.

wHOOOSH!

Butterfly and Ermine shot
through the end of the wave
and glided elegantly onto the
beach to wild applause from
the other competitors.

CRASH!

The wave finally broke.
A massive dump of churning white
surf swallowed the paddle boat, rolling
it over and over and over on the sand.
Winifred and Cruella staggered
from the sea and collapsed.

They looked terrible. Winifred's wetsuit
ballooned with water. Her wig was on backwards
(not to mention her underwear). Cruella's short
fur was plastered with evil-smelling seaweed. A
small crab was attached to one ear.

Winifred spat the sand out of her mouth.
"That's IT," she fumed. "It's time to play
dirty."

Chapter 8

The next morning, back at Sylvia's house...

Sydney
AUSTRALIA

Er-mazing
Ermine!

Super stoat set for stardom!

Ermine sat at the table, pasting photos into her scrapbook. The newspapers were full of her success at the Junior Super Surfer Competition the day before.

Ermine sighed. All the newspapers said she and Butterfly were bound to win *Australia's Most Awesome Animal Show*. There was just one small problem: the competition was that afternoon at two thirty and she and Butterfly still hadn't decided on their act. None of their talents seemed quite right for the show. Acrobatics was out. So was fishing and cooking. And even though they were both *spectacularly* good at surfing, they couldn't very well do that onstage, or sledding for that matter as there wasn't any snow.

Just then Butterfly came into the kitchen. She was wearing pajamas, a baseball cap, mismatched slippers and a big frown from having been woken up early by Sylvia. She plonked herself down at the table and reached for the cereal. Then she removed Ermine's list of talents from under her cap.

☒ Climbing
☒ Fishing
☒ Swimming
☒ Sledding
☐ Fixing bicycles
☐ Solving diamond robberies

"What about fixing bicycles?" Ermine said. "I'm pretty good at that."

"**Boring!**" said Butterfly. "And there aren't any diamond robberies to solve." She crossed those out as well. "What else could we do?"

Ermine thought about all the things the Duchess had taught her. "We could show people how to put up shelves," she suggested, "or polish a table with beeswax or make a feathered hat."

"Even **more** **boring!**" said Butterfly.

Ermine frowned. Butterfly was in a bad mood. The Duchess called it "getting out of bed on the wrong side."

"What about breakdancing?" said Butterfly.

"That's a good idea," Ermine said. "Stoats are **fantastic** at dancing."

"Says who?" said Butterfly curiously.

"Lots of people," Ermine replied.

"Like who?" Butterfly insisted.

"Like…" Ermine tried to think.

Wait a minute! Her black eyes gleamed with excitement. *Of course!* She knew exactly what they could do for the show – Butterfly had given her a **fantastic** idea.

"LIKE ERIC!" she squeaked. "That's IT, Butterfly! We can ask Eric to play for us at the show while we dance." She did a cartwheel across the kitchen table.

"Who's Eric?" asked Butterfly.

"The man I met on the quay when you went to get the notepad at the cafe," Ermine explained. "He plays the didgeridoo. It's the sound of nature. That's why I liked it so much – it reminded me of the forest in Balaclavia. So I started dancing and Eric said I was pretty good for a weasel and I told him I was a **stoat** and everyone clapped."

"Why on earth didn't you say so before, silly?" cried Butterfly. "That sounds amazing. I'll get Grandma." She rushed off upstairs.

Just then Ermine heard something drop through the letter box in the hall. She went to pick it up. To her surprise, the envelope was addressed to her. She slit it open with her claw and pulled out a piece of thick white paper.

Ermine blinked. It was from Winifred
Winnit.

Dear Ermine,

Welcome to Sydney!
I am ~~dead livid~~ delighted that you are taking
~~over~~ part in Australia's Most Awesome Animal
Show this year. Seeing as how you were brought
up by a duchess and can talk (~~curse~~ clever you!),
me and my pet Tasmanian devil, Cruella,
would like to ~~eat~~ meet you before the show.
Come to the ~~cage~~ stage door at 2 p.m.
The wallabies are quite ~~tiresome~~ timid,
so please come alone. Don't tell ~~Caterpillar~~
Butterfly.
   Catch you soon!
   Winifred Winnit

PS Sorry I am not very good at ~~singing~~ spelling.

Ermine wondered what she should do. On the one paw, Butterfly would be disappointed not to meet Winifred and the wallabies before they went onstage, but on the other paw, Ermine really wanted to go. She decided she would – it would only take two minutes and she could ask Winifred for an autograph to give to Butterfly as a surprise.

"Ready?" Butterfly appeared in the doorway with Sylvia.

Ermine stuffed the letter in her pocket guiltily. She grabbed her straw hat, threw her camera over one shoulder and picked up her tool bag. "Ready!" she said.

A little while later, Sylvia, Butterfly and Ermine got off the ferry at the quay.

Ermine looked around anxiously for Eric.

NYOW-WOW-WA-NYOW-WOW-WA-NYOW-WOW-WA!

The sound of the didgeridoo reverberated along her whiskers.

"There he is!" Ermine scurried over to where Eric was entertaining a large crowd. She pushed her way to the front of the group with

Butterfly. They both found their feet tapping in time to the rhythm.

"**Ermine!**" Eric cried when he finished the song. "It's good to see you again! And you must be Butterfly…"

"How do you know that?" asked Butterfly.

Eric smiled. "I've been reading about you in the news. You two are pretty popular around here at the moment. Now what can I do for you?"

"We want you to play for us at *Australia's Most Awesome Animal Show*." Ermine explained her idea to Eric.

"**Pleeeeeeaaaaaaase!**" said Butterfly, when Ermine had finished.

"No worries," Eric said. "I'd be glad to." He picked up the didgeridoo and followed Butterfly and Ermine to where Sylvia was waiting.

Ermine made the introductions. "Sylvia, meet Eric. Eric, meet Sylvia. Sylvia's the world's greatest opera singer," she added by way of explanation. "And Eric's the world's greatest didgeridoo player."

The two grown-ups greeted each other warmly.

"I'm so glad you agreed to play for them," said Sylvia to Eric. "Your music will sound wonderful in the concert hall."

They made their way along the promenade to the Opera House and up the steps. There was a big line of people waiting to collect their tickets. They waved to Ermine and Butterfly. Ermine and Butterfly waved back. Butterfly even signed a few autographs.

The attendant showed them into the concert hall.

Ermine gasped when she saw inside. The hall was like a great cathedral, with rows and rows and rows of seats all around, a huge organ at the back and a fan-shaped roof flooded with light. In front of them was an enormous stage with an orchestra pit below.

"It's amazing," she whispered. "You know, Butterfly, you really *should* go to the opera one day and hear your grandma sing."

"Oh, all right," Butterfly said. "But I'm not going to wear a feathered hat."

The concert hall was filling up quickly. "This way." The attendant showed them to the front, where seats had been reserved for them behind the judges. Most of the other competitors were already there.

Paul Piggott and Pete the
percussion-playing platypus

Lucy Sponge and
Sue the sighing sloth

Bill Trogg and Bert
the bearded tarantula

The only ones missing were Winifred
Winnit and her performing wallabies.

★ WINIFRED WINNIT ★

★ WALLABY 1 ★

★ WALLABY 2 ★

★ WALLABY 3 ★

They must be waiting for me, thought Ermine. "Back in a minute," she said to Butterfly, wiggling off her seat.

"Where are you going?" Butterfly asked suspiciously.

"To the ladies room," Ermine lied. "I need to…ah…wash my whiskers." She scurried off before Butterfly and Sylvia had a chance to stop her.

Sylvia and Butterfly exchanged glances.

"Why do I get the feeling she's up to something?" Sylvia said.

"I'm not sure, but so do I," Butterfly replied. She got out of her seat. "Don't worry, Grandma, you wait there. I'll make sure she's okay."

Chapter 9

At the stage door of the Sydney Opera House...

Winifred Winnit was
waiting for Ermine
at the stage door. She was
wearing her colorful
clown outfit with a pair
of enormous red shoes
and long, candy-striped laces.

"Sorry I'm late!" Ermine panted.

"Never mind!"
tinkled Winifred.

"Come and say hello to the team." She led the way to her dressing room, ushered Ermine inside and closed the door firmly behind her.

Ermine was surprised to see the wallabies were penned up in a cage. She was also surprised to see a creature the size of a small dog wearing a gold collar keeping watch on them.

It had a bandage on its nose.

"This is Cruella," Winifred said.

Ermine stared hard at Cruella. There was something familiar about the animal's great jaws and long toes. Come to think of it, there was something familiar about Winifred too.

She peered at her closely.

Underneath Winifred's makeup were traces of black ink.

Then she realized. **Winifred and Cruella were the surfer dude and his dog!** "You were at the aquarium!" she gasped.

Winifred nodded. Her expression had changed. She was looking at Ermine as if she'd just eaten a super-sour piece of candy. Ermine felt a little worried. Something told her that Winifred wasn't very pleased to see her after all.

There was an awkward pause.

"I'm sorry about squirting squid ink in your eyes," Ermine said eventually.

"*Are* you?" said Winifred heavily. "What about **squelching** me with a sea cucumber?"

"And that," said Ermine. "Although you must admit it was a silly place to stand."

Winifred glowered at her. "What about using my backside as a pincushion for sea urchins?"

"Now that wasn't my fault..." Ermine began.

AND PRACTICALLY DROWNING ME AT THE SURF COMPETITION?

Winifred's voice rose to a scream. It echoed around the dressing room.

"*Did* I?" Ermine said in a puzzled voice. "I'm afraid I didn't notice. I was having so much fun."

Just then the door flew open. It was Butterfly. She'd been listening through the keyhole.

"What are *you* doing here?" demanded Winifred.

"Never mind that," said Butterfly hotly. "The question is what were *you* doing following *us*? And why were you in disguise?"

"We were trying to catch your little ferrety friend, of course!" Winifred said.

Ermine's whiskers twitched with annoyance. She didn't take kindly to being compared with a ferret. "You mean *me*, I suppose?" she said haughtily. Suddenly she remembered the Duke. "You don't want to make me into a fur collar, do you? It's a bit hot for that in Australia, I should say."

Winifred shook her head. "No. I just want you out of the way so that I can be crowned winner of *Australia's Most Awesome Animal Show* one last time, like I deserve." She gave an evil laugh. "Then I can buy a Jacuzzi and finally get rid of these loathsome wallabies."

"You mean you don't like wallabies?" Butterfly said, horrified.

"I HATE wallabies," said Winifred. "And koalas. If one ever kissed me, I'd be SICK. That goes for stoats too, although you *would* make an excellent duster." She made a grab for Ermine. "Easy peasy, Ermine squeezy!" she cried.

Ermine dodged out of the way.

"COME HERE!" Winifred screamed. "I WANT YOU TO CLEAN MY HOUSE!"

She made another lunge for Ermine, tripped over her enormous shoes and fell hard on her bottom.

"QUICK, ERMINE, RUN!" shouted Butterfly, holding open the door.

"In a minute!" said Ermine. "First I'm letting the wallabies out."

She scampered past Winifred,

somersaulted off
Cruella's back

and climbed
up the bars
of the cage.

She felt in
her tool bag
and pulled
out a pair of
wire cutters.

"WATCH OUT FOR CRUELLA, ERMINE!"

Butterfly cried.

Ermine glanced around. The Tasmanian devil was just behind her. Clinging on to the wire she grasped the cutters in one paw.

SNIP!

The padlocks fell to the floor and the cage door swung open on Cruella, sending her hurtling into Winifred's lap.

The wallabies bounced out.

Winifred let out a shriek of rage.

"Follow me, wallabies!" Ermine led the way out of the dressing room and along the corridor. Butterfly raced after her with the wallabies. They rushed into the concert hall and onto the stage.

"HURRY, CRUELLA!" Winifred lumbered after them in her enormous shoes, the Tasmanian devil close behind.

Bill Trogg and his bearded
tarantula were just finishing their act.
"LOOK OUT FOR BERT!" shouted Bill,
as Winifred mounted the steps.

But it was too late. Winifred's long laces
had become tangled up with the
tarantula's beard. She tripped
over again. This time she
landed face down in the
middle of the stage in
front of the audience.

The tarantula untangled its
beard from her laces and crawled
up her clown suit into her hair.
The audience gasped.

"GET THE STOAT,
CRUELLA!"
Winifred cried.

The audience froze in shock. They couldn't believe what they were seeing. Cameras zoomed in from every angle. All across Australia, the nation was glued to their TV screens.

Cruella advanced on Ermine.

Ermine zigzagged this way and that, but the stage was so crowded with people and wallabies, not to mention Winifred and her enormous shoes she couldn't escape.

"GGGGRRRRRRRRR!"

Cruella opened her great jaws.

"WALLABIES! HELP ERMINE!"

Butterfly cried.

BOING! BOING! BOING!

The wallabies surrounded Cruella, making a tight fence around her with their broad tails.

Cruella growled and
growled, but the wallabies
didn't budge. Now Ermine
and Butterfly had come to their
rescue, they were no longer afraid
of Cruella.

One of the wallabies
gave her a big KICK.
Cruella flew
through the air...

and landed
safely in one of the
drums in the orchestra pit.

"I'LL GET YOU FOR THIS!" Winifred shrieked. She struggled to her feet, the tarantula still on her head, and parted its beard from her eyes. She staggered towards Ermine. "Get out of my way, wallabies," she hissed. "I want that STOAT. This is my competition. MINE!"

Ermine ran up the tail of the biggest wallaby and somersaulted onto its head. "DON'T LISTEN TO HER, WALLABIES!" she shouted.

"This is <u>your</u> competition, not Winifred Winnit's. <u>You're</u> the ones the audience wants to see!"

The audience clapped and cheered. Ermine was right. No one cared about Winifred any more.

To Winifred's astonishment the wallabies pushed past her to the front of the stage and began to **dance**.

Only it wasn't the dance Winifred had taught them. It was the sort of dance they would do together in the wild.

They **tumbled** and **bounced**.

They **twisted** and **sprang**.

They even started **play-boxing**.

They were enjoying themselves so much
that one of them accidentally biffed Winifred
on the nose!

Winifred tripped over for a third time.
She fell off the stage and landed in the drum
with Cruella.

"AAAARRRRRRGGHHHHH!"
she screamed.

Everyone in the audience
started to laugh.

Butterfly giggled
helplessly.

Ermine leaped from the wallaby's head onto Butterfly's shoulder, pulled out her camera and pointed it towards Winifred. "You don't mind if I get a photo for my scrapbook, do you?" she said with a winning smile. "The Duchess did say I have to fill it up."

SNAP! FLASH!

"*And now, ladies and gentlemen, the act you have all been waiting for,*" said the presenter. "*From Balaclavia, dancing to the didgeridoo, here's Ermine with her special friends, Eric and Butterfly!*"

Eric came up onstage beside Ermine and Butterfly. The wallabies took a bow. Eric placed his didgeridoo in front of him and began to play.

NYOW-WOW-WA-NYOW-WOW-WA-NYOW-WOW-WA

The sound of nature echoed around the concert hall.

Ermine flipped and cartwheeled. She somersaulted and jived. She even did the worm. Butterfly joined in. So did the wallabies and all the other animals in the show. Together they danced and danced to Eric's wonderful music, to the delight of the cheering crowd.

Dear Duchess,

I am having a fantastic time in Sydney. I have made great friends with Sylvia and Butterfly (especially since I rescued Butterfly from Sydney Harbor Bridge). Butterfly is very independent-minded (like me). She has finally agreed to go to the opera tonight to hear Sylvia sing with Luciano Singalotti, although (unlike me) she refuses to wear a feathered hat.

You might have seen on the news that Butterfly and I won Australia's Most Awesome Animal Show thanks to an amazing musician named Eric, who is the world's greatest didgeridoo player. It turns out that last year's winner – Winifred Winnit – didn't even like animals! She tried to stop me from taking part, but my new friends the wallabies came to the rescue just in time and booted Winifred and her horrible pet Tasmanian devil into a drum in the orchestra pit.

Sylvia suggested that I should give the prize money from the show to the Opera House to spend on more projects with Eric and his friends, which I think is a very good idea – but don't worry, I have set aside enough to buy you a present. I thought you might like one of Eric's CDs!

I have also taken lots of photographs and am keeping up-to-date with my scrapbook.

Lots of love, Ermine

PS. Please could you write and tell me where I'm going next on my travels? I think I fancy somewhere with a lot of history...

AUSTRALIA

SYDNEY
★ ★ ★
POSTAGE

AUSTRALIA

POSTAGE PAID

Grand Duchess Maria Von Schnitzel

The Imperial House of Hasbeen

Hasbeen Castle

Balaclavia

Europe

THE TRAVELS OF

Ermine

The Big London Treasure Hunt

Ermine's Top Tips

London was first built nearly 2,000 years ago, when the Roman army invaded Britain. They built a town beside the River Thames, and named it **Londinium**. Nowadays, as Ermine and Minty discover, London is filled to the brim with things to see and do. Here are **Ermine's top tips** for sightseeing in the city!

Marvel at the Crown Jewels

Ever wanted to see the crowns and jewels that British kings and queens have worn for the past 600 years? Then head to the Tower of London! And, not just that, but you can also visit the prison that housed lots of historical prisoners, including Henry VIII's wife, Anne Boleyn. Can you spot a Beefeater and a raven while you're there?

Travel in style on a river cruise!

Like Ermine and Minty, you can jump aboard a boat to take in the sights of London by water... With routes from Putney to Greenwich and Richmond to Hampton Court, you can travel the River Thames like a Tudor monarch.

for Visiting London

Get lost in the Hampton Court Palace maze

And where better to end up than the Hampton Court Palace maze? The maze is legendary for bamboozling visitors with its twists and turns. It's the oldest surviving maze in all of England! Can you puzzle your way to the middle? (But watch out for those bees!)

Discover what Shakespeare's London might have felt like at the Globe

Ever wondered what it might have been like to go to the theater in Tudor times? At the Globe, you can jump into the past and see where Shakespeare's plays were first performed. Wow!

Take to the skies on the London Eye!

And for something more modern, you can ride the ENORMOUS Ferris wheel on London's Southbank! Can you spot all the sights that Ermine and Minty visit from the sky?

The Travels of Ermine

LONDON
UK

EUROPE

NORTH
AMERICA

NEW
YORK

AFRICA

PACIFIC
OCEAN

ATLANTIC
OCEAN

SOUTH
AMERICA

SOUTHERN
OCEAN

ANTARCTICA

Ermine

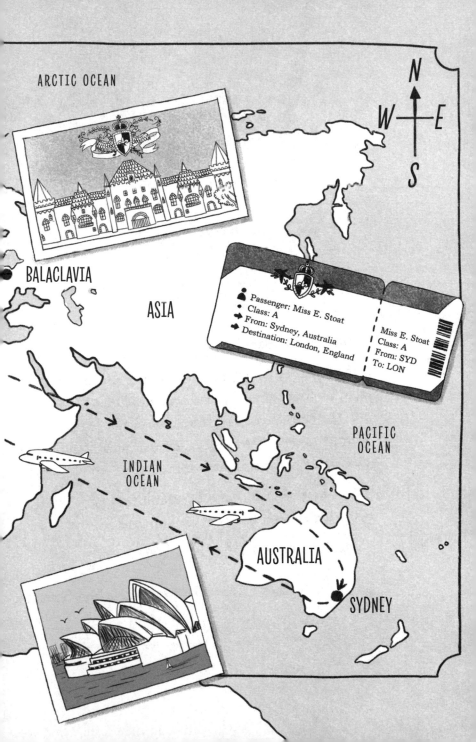

Dear Tom and Rani,

Thank you for your kind invitation to have Ermine to stay in London on her world travels. Since I adopted her, she has become very interested in history and wants to learn more about kings and queens, especially as Balaclavia doesn't have them any more.

I'm sure she will have a brilliant time with Minty – the two of them have so much in common!

With best wishes,

Maria Grand Duchess Maria Von Schnitzel

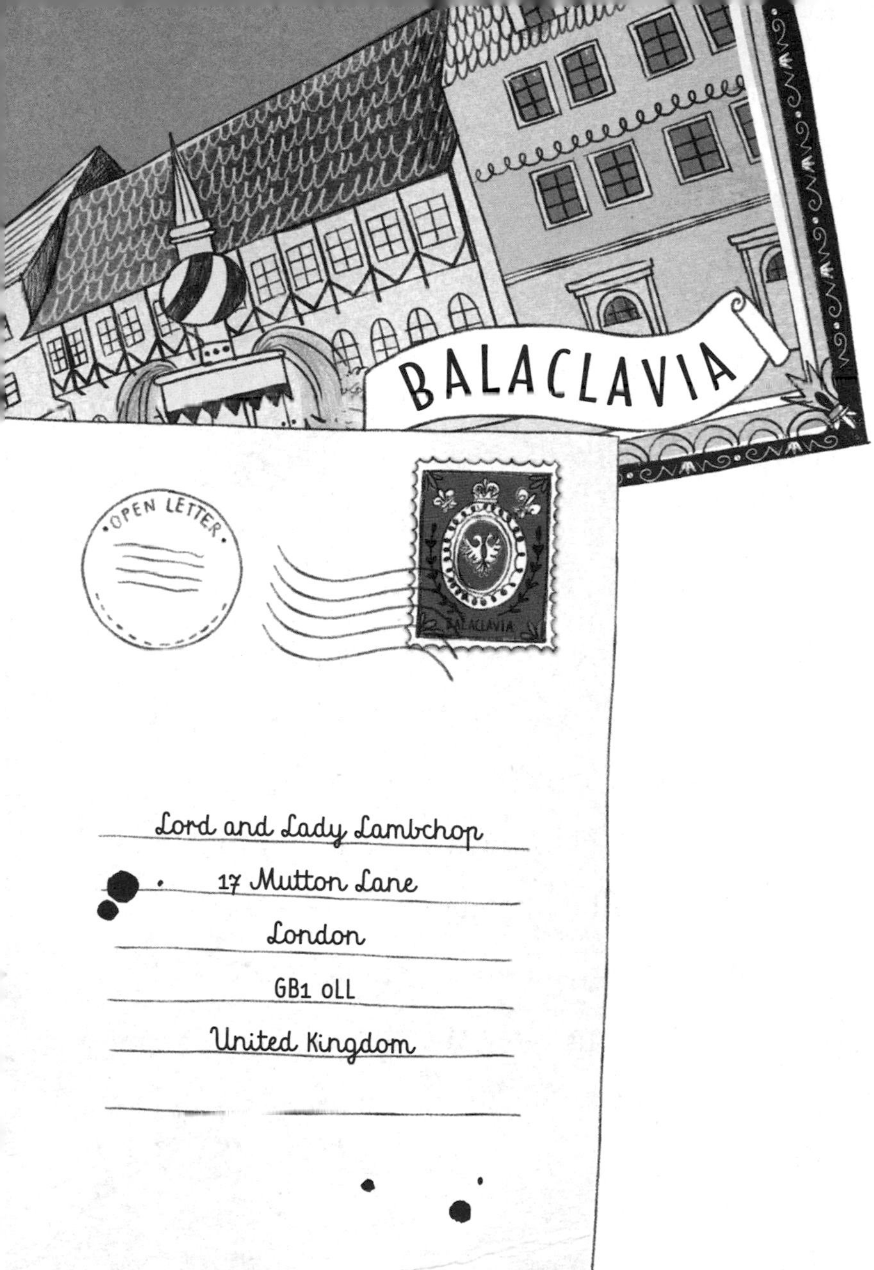
BALACLAVIA
OPEN LETTER
BALACLAVIA
Lord and Lady Lambchop
17 Mutton Lane
London
GB1 oLL
United Kingdom

Chapter 1

The City of London...

It was summer vacation and Minty
Lambchop was up and dressed early.
She couldn't wait for their visitor to arrive.

Minty was eight years old. She had brown
eyes and thick black curly hair tied into two
even pigtails. She had chosen her clothes
carefully: blue denim overalls, white
T-shirt and new sneakers. She
wanted to make a good
impression.

Minty sat on her bed, staring out of the window expectantly. School vacations (especially summer ones) always *sounded* like a great idea, but now they were into week four and she was beginning to feel restless. Not that she wanted to go back to school yet – it was just that their house was a bit, well, CROWDED.

Despite being a lord and lady, Minty's parents – Tom and Rani – didn't have pots of money. The Lambchops' home was a tall topsy-turvy sort of house surrounded by other tall topsy-turvy houses on a narrow street in the heart of the old City of London.

Lord Lambchop
worked in the
basement. Lady
Lambchop
worked in
the attic. In
between, there
was a kitchen,
a sitting room,
three bedrooms
and a bathroom,
not to mention
several flights of
very steep stairs.
And at the back
was a tiny
garden.

Minty's dad, Tom, was a conservationist. When he wasn't at home (like now), he was in far-off places exploring the deepest, darkest jungle. Big cats were Minty's dad's passion. But as he couldn't very well keep big jungle cats in a crowded London house, he kept domestic ones instead.

Minty's mom, Rani, was a children's author. She wrote books about a detective named **Polly Potter** and her trusty sidekick, Mable the talking parrot. When she wasn't writing, Minty's mom was reading. And when she wasn't reading, she and Minty helped Lord Lambchop look after his army of stray cats.

Minty loved reading too, especially detective stories. When she grew up, she wanted to be a famous sleuth and solve lots of mysteries, like Sherlock Holmes. She thought Polly Potter was **awesome**. She'd read all the **Polly Potter** books. She'd pinned **Polly Potter** posters on her bedroom walls. She had a **Polly Potter** bedspread. She was even the proud owner of a limited edition **Polly Potter Detective Set**. The only thing she didn't have was a talking parrot.

But if what her mom had said was true, then she might be about to receive a visit from someone even better…

Just then, through the window, she spotted a black taxi appearing at the end of the little street. Minty jumped off her bed, flew down the stairs, and opened the front door.

The taxi drew up at the curb. The driver got out and held open the passenger door. Out stepped a small, brown, furry animal with a long, bushy, black-tipped tail, two coal-black eyes, white whiskers and a pink nose. The creature was wearing a pinafore dress the same color as Minty's overalls and a mustard-yellow waterproof hat. A Polaroid camera was slung over one shoulder. In one paw it carried an umbrella and in the other a small bag marked TOOL BAG.

"Thank you," it said politely to the driver. Then it turned around and waved its umbrella at Minty.

"Hello," it said brightly.
"I'm Ermine. You must
be Minty."

Minty blinked.
So it WAS true what
her mom had said.
Their visitor really
could talk.

Move over Polly Potter and Mable, Minty thought, *here comes Minty Lambchop and Ermine, the talking stoat.* Minty felt even more excited – they were going to have an **amazing** time together, especially if they could find a mystery to solve! "Ermine!" she cried. Ermine dashed up the front steps. The taxi driver trailed after her, carrying a very large number of very small suitcases, which he deposited in a pile.

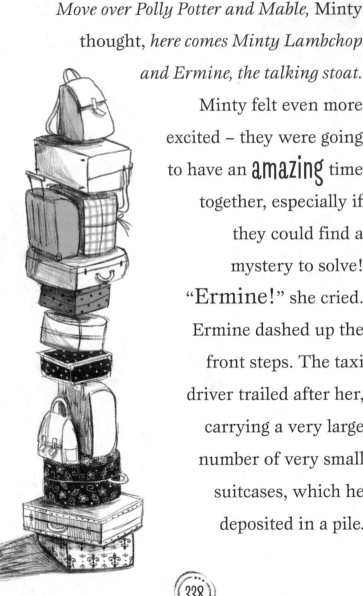

Ermine placed the umbrella on the floor and removed her waterproof hat. "I brought these in case it rains," she said. "The Duchess said it *always* rains in London."

"It does rain *quite* a lot," Minty said carefully. She didn't like to tell their visitor that they were actually in the middle of a summer heatwave.

"We don't get much rain in Balaclavia," Ermine continued. (The Duchess had also told her that British people love talking about the weather.) "It's hot in the summer and it snows in the winter. That's when my fur changes color from brown to white, so other animals can't see me."

"Awesome," said Minty. Being a master of disguise was an important part of detective work and it occurred to her that having a sidekick who could camouflage herself might prove very useful.

"Thank you," Ermine said. She gave a little sigh. "Although it didn't stop the Duke from trying to catch me."

"The Duke?" Minty echoed.

"The Duchess's husband," Ermine explained sadly. "He wanted to use my fur to trim his robes – the ones he used to wear in the old days when Balaclavia had a king. It's very precious, my fur. It's called ermine, like me. Luckily the Duchess came to the rescue. She told the Duke that the only place for ermine was on a stoat and adopted me instead."

"That *was* lucky," Minty, who was also adopted, agreed. The Duchess was right: the two of them really did have a lot in common.

They were going to be great friends.

Ermine nodded. "The Duchess taught me lots of useful things, like how to use a wrench and when to wear a feathered hat. And then she sent me on my world travels, so that I could meet new people and visit interesting places."

"That's a really good idea!" said Minty, thinking she'd like to do the same one day.

Ermine looked around anxiously. "Minty, do your mom and dad have robes?" she whispered.

"I don't *think* so," Minty whispered back. "They're not really that grand."

"How come?" Ermine sounded surprised. "They're a lord and lady, aren't they?"

"Yes, but that doesn't mean they're rich," said Minty. "Mom and Dad both work for a living." She explained what each of them did.

"You mean they don't get money from the Queen?" Ermine asked, puzzled.

Minty shook her head. "No. It doesn't work like that."

"What, not even in the old days?" Ermine insisted. It sounded very different from Balaclavia, where the King used to dish out money to all his favorites, like the Duke.

"Well, Dad's ancestor, Larkin Lambchop, *was* given some treasure, once upon a time," said Minty.

"So what happened to it?" said Ermine, looking around.

"It vanished," Minty said.

"Vanished?" repeated Ermine, intrigued.

"Yes," said Minty. "The mystery of the Lambchop treasure is one of the great unsolved crimes in British history."

Ermine's face set into a very determined expression. "Then *we* should find it, Minty!" she cried. "So your mom can write a book about it and your dad can put the money towards saving jungle cats." Her whiskers twitched in excitement. "And *we* can go down in history as the ones who finally solved the mystery."

Minty gave a whoop. "That's a **brilliant** idea, Ermine!" The lost treasure of the Lambchops was the *perfect* mystery for them to solve together.

Ermine clapped her paws together. *A treasure hunt!* It felt like the start of another **stoat-ily thrilling adventure!**

introducing
Minty Lambchop & Ermine
in The Mystery of the Lost Treasure

Chapter 2

At Ye Olde Tudor Cafe...

A little while later Ermine and Minty sat with Lady Lambchop around a small wooden table in a nearby cafe.

The cafe was in a ramshackle black-and-white building with stained-glass windows overlooking the River Thames. The cafe looked very old, especially compared to all the shiny new buildings surrounding it.

"It's been here since Elizabethan times," Lady Lambchop explained. Rani Lambchop

was a tall elegant woman with long dark hair,
a ready smile and (Ermine thought) a daring
choice of hat for the notoriously unpredictable
British weather – a big straw one with a wide
pink ribbon. Despite Ermine's concerns that it
might rain, the sun was still shining brightly.

"And that's the Globe Theatre – where
Shakespeare's plays are performed," said Lady

Lambchop, pointing through the open window.

The Globe Theatre also looked very old,
like the cafe. It was round in shape, painted
white on the outside, with thick dark wooden
beams, tiny windows and a thatched roof.
Ermine took a couple of snapshots with her
camera to put in her scrapbook, while Minty
told her mom about their plan to be detectives.

"A **treasure hunt?**" Lady Lambchop exclaimed. "What a good idea, Ermine!"

"Thank you," said Ermine distractedly. She was busy studying the menu on the blackboard.

Main course
Roast beef
& Yorkshire pudding
Fish and Chips
Pie and mash
Toad-in-the-hole
Bubble and squeak

Dessert
Bread-and-butter pudding
Jelly and ice cream
Iced buns

Ermine found the menu very confusing. She had never been anywhere where they ate pudding for a main course and bread and butter for dessert before.

But there was one thing on the menu that really puzzled her.

"Isn't that a bit YUCKY?" she asked, scratching her head.

"Isn't what a bit yucky?" said Minty.

"Toad," said Ermine. "Especially if you serve it in its own hole." She made a face, imagining a plateful of green toad served up on a bed of mud.

Minty giggled. "It's not a *real* toad, Ermine!" she said. "It's sausages in batter."

"*Toad* sausages?!" Ermine asked.

Minty giggled even more. "No! Ordinary sausages. It's got nothing to do with toads."

"Then why is it called toad-in-the-hole?" Ermine demanded hotly. How was she supposed to know that toad-in-the-hole was another name for a battered sausage?

Lady Lambchop came to the rescue. "I think it's called that because the sausages peek out of the batter, like toads peeking out of their holes," she said.

"Oh," said Ermine. She supposed that sort of made sense. Her eyes traveled back down the blackboard. "I didn't know you could eat bubbles and squeaks. What do they taste like?"

Minty laughed helplessly. "It's not *real* bubbles and squeaks," she said. "It's leftover cabbage and potato fried up together."

Ermine frowned. She wasn't sure she'd ever get the hang of British food. "What about the iced buns?" she asked. "Are they cold enough to make my fur turn white?"

"No!" said Minty. "They're not cold at all. The iced part is just the sticky stuff on top."

"Why don't I order for you, Ermine?" suggested Lady Lambchop.

"I think that would be a very good idea." Ermine sighed.

The waiter came over. "Three fish and chips, please," said Lady Lambchop. She poured everyone a cup of tea from a large teapot. "Now, Ermine, if you're going to solve

the mystery of the Lambchop treasure, you
need to know the story of Larkin Lambchop,"
she said. "It's called the Great Pastry Plot."

The Great Pastry Plot. It sounded thrilling!

"Ooh, ooh, ooh," squeaked Ermine.
"I love history." She cupped her chin in her
paws and rested her elbows on the table.

"It all started
back in 1565,"
said Lady
Lambchop,

"when Elizabeth I was the Queen of England. Elizabeth was one of a great dynasty of kings and queens called the Tudors…"

Ermine listened hard.

"She was the daughter of King Henry VIII—"

"Wasn't he very large?" Ermine interrupted, remembering a picture she'd seen in her London guidebook.

"He was when he got old," Minty told her.

"He probably ate too much bread and butter for pudding," said Ermine.

"Quite possibly," agreed Lady Lambchop.

QUEEN ELIZABETH I

"Anyway, after Henry died and Elizabeth became queen, she used to visit her father's old palace at Hampton Court. It's in a beautiful spot on the River Thames and Henry VIII built great kitchens there so he could entertain kings and queens from all over Europe…"

"Wait a minute, Mum. I need to write this down so we remember it all." Minty opened her Polly Potter Detective Set and took out a notebook and pen. She began to make notes.

"In those days, the Lambchop family worked in the kitchens," said Lady Lambchop. "The youngest of them, Larkin, turned the meat on the roasting spit. One day, when Queen Elizabeth was entertaining the French Ambassador, he noticed something very suspicious…"

Ermine felt a shiver run through her.

"While all the other cooks were taking the feast up to the Queen and her guests in the great gallery above, Larkin Lambchop saw one of the Queen's closest advisers – Lord William

Wellington – sneak through the roasting kitchen and pour poison in the Queen's pie."

"No!" gasped Ermine. Pouring poison in the Queen's pie was a terrible thing to do. "Why did he do that?"

"The Queen didn't have any children," Lady Lambchop explained. "Lord Wellington thought that if he poisoned her, *he* could seize the throne. But luckily Larkin Lambchop raised the alarm just in time."

NO!
WAIT!

"What happened then?" asked Minty.

"The Queen was so angry with Lord William Wellington that she stripped him of his title on the spot, confiscated all his riches and ordered him to be imprisoned for treason," said Lady Lambchop. "And she was so grateful to Larkin Lambchop that she made *him* a lord instead and bestowed on him a priceless ruby from her very own crown."

Minty scribbled furiously.

"But the guards weren't paying attention," said Lady Lambchop. "Just as the Queen was handing Larkin Lambchop the ruby, Lord Wellington sprang from his captors and snatched it from Her Majesty's grasp. Somehow Wellington managed to escape. By the time he was recaptured the next day, the ruby had vanished."

Ermine was on the edge of her seat. It was one of the best stories she had ever heard.

"So, you see," said Lady Lambchop, "although the title has been passed down over the centuries through the Lambchop family, the whereabouts of the ruby remain a complete mystery…" She paused. "Although *some* say Wellington left a set of clues."

Clues! Minty put down her pen. She grinned at Ermine. This was definitely a job for Minty Lambchop and her trusty sidekick, Ermine!

Ermine grinned back. She couldn't wait to get going with *her* trusty sidekick, Minty!

Just then the waiter placed three platefuls of golden fish and chips in front of them. Ermine sniffed cautiously. To her relief, it smelled absolutely delicious. Maybe British food wasn't so bad after all!

She nibbled delicately on a piping-hot chip.

"There's only one thing to do," said Minty. "We need to find those clues, Ermine!"

"You could start at Hampton Court," Lady Lambchop suggested.

Hampton Court. Ermine chewed thoughtfully on a forkful of steaming white fish and crunchy batter. Her eyes fell on the river. "How about we take a boat?" she said.

Chapter 3

In some barracks near Buckingham Palace...

Corporal Bertram ("Beef") Wellington and his horse, Radish, had just finished a long morning on parade. Now they were back in the stable next to the barracks where the Queen's cavalry lived.

The Corporal sat on a small three-legged stool, polishing his boots. Radish stood next to him, tethered to his stall with his nose in a bag of hay. Corporal Wellington was still wearing part of his ceremonial uniform – white jodhpurs and a scarlet tunic with silver buttons. The rest of it lay on a rack beside him. He had

already spent an hour polishing
his silver helmet, breastplate and
sword. But the thigh-length
riding boots were by far the worst.

He regarded them gloomily.
The boots glistened like
coal. But glistening like
coal wasn't good enough
for Quartermaster
Grouch. They had to
twinkle like stars.

The stable door banged
loudly. Footsteps pounded
on the cobbles.

LEFT. RIGHT.
LEFT. RIGHT. LEFT. RIGHT.

Beef Wellington gave a deep sigh.

Speak of the devil…

Quartermaster Grouch marched over and lunged towards him. "GIVE IT SOME WELLY, WELLINGTON!" he shouted. (Quartermaster Grouch always shouted, even when his mouth was an inch away from your ear.)

Beef Wellington's eardrums vibrated painfully. But it didn't do to disobey Quartermaster Grouch. The Quartermaster had all manner of cruel and unusual punishments for soldiers who disobeyed his orders.

"Yes, sir!" he said meekly, buffing the boots furiously.

"HOW MANY TIMES DO I HAVE TO TELL YOU? THOSE BOOTS SHOULD BE TWINKLING LIKE STARS, NOT GLISTENING LIKE COAL!" bellowed Quartermaster Grouch.

"Yes, sir!"

Quartermaster Grouch stood up. He took a long, hard look at Radish's gleaming flank. "And when you're done with that you can groom your horse properly. It's got dust on its coat."

"But…" Beef Wellington clamped his mouth shut. He'd been about to point out to the Quartermaster that it was impossible for a large, jet-black horse to stand in a stable full of sawdust without getting dust on its coat, before he realized his mistake.

But it was too late.

Quartermaster Grouch's throat began to rumble like an erupting volcano.

Beef Wellington braced himself.

He was in for it now!

DID I HEAR YOU SAY BUT?

the Quartermaster roared.

"No, sir!" Beef Wellington lied.

Quartermaster Grouch's face was scarlet, like his tunic. "BECAUSE IF I DID, LADDIE, YOU'RE FOR THE CHOP. THERE'LL BE NO SNAKES AND LADDERS AFTER TEA FOR YOU TONIGHT." (No snakes and ladders after tea was one of the Quartermaster's favorite cruel and unusual punishments.) "GOT THAT, WELLINGTON?"

"Got it, sir."

The Quartermaster clicked his heels, marched back along the cobbles LEFT. RIGHT. LEFT. RIGHT. LEFT. RIGHT. and slammed the stable door.

Beef Wellington glared daggers after him. It was bad enough not being allowed to play snakes and ladders after tea with the rest of the regiment, but it was the use of the word "chop" that really enraged him.

"Chop!" he muttered, grinding his teeth.

"Chop!" he choked, rolling the word around his mouth and spitting it out like a bad banana.

"Chop, chop, *chop,* CHOP, <u>CHOP!</u>" His voice rose to a scream.

Radish stopped chewing and wiggled his nose out of the nosebag. He whinnied.

Beef Wellington pummeled his boots with the polishing cloth. "I should be the one giving orders and dishing out cruel and unusual punishments around here, not Quartermaster Grouch," he fumed. "And that's not all…"

Radish drew his lips back from his teeth and made an ugly face. He knew what was coming.

"I shouldn't be a corporal – I should be a lord! *Lord* Bertram 'Beef' Wellington: Head of the Household Cavalry, Knight of the Garter, Great Master of the Most Honorable Order of the Bathtub, Leader of the Noble Society of Silk Socks, Guardian of the Queen's Chamber Pot,

Chief Taster of Royal Pies, Collector in Residence of the Queen's Toenail Clippings…"

Corporal Beef Wellington reeled off a great long list of things he ought to be in charge of.

Radish snorted impatiently. He'd heard it all before.

"It's *true,* Radish," his keeper insisted. "Us Wellingtons have a proud history. I've been doing some more research online – look." Beef Wellington pulled a piece of paper from his pocket and spread it out on his knee.

Radish eyed it hungrily.

"It's not food, Radish, it's family," Beef Wellington said crossly.

THE LORD WELLINGTONS

of Britain

WILLARD THE WELLINGTON
(founder of the Wellington dynasty)
1066 – 1123

LORD WINSTON WELLINGTON
(the wise) 1169 – 1237

LORD WILBERFORCE WELLINGTON
(the stupid) 1237 – 1301

WALLACE WELLINGTON
(the brave) 1123 – 1169

LORD WISHFUL WELLINGTON
(the hopeful) 1301 – 1360

LORD WOEBEGONE WELLINGTON
(the hopeless) 1360 – 1412

LORD WALTER WELLINGTON
(the old) 1412 – 1513

LORD WALTER WELLINGTON
(the young) 1513 – 1515

LORD LARKIN LAMBCHOP
(the noble)

LORD WILLIAM WELLINGTON
(THE TRAITOR) 1515 – 1565

And his descendants (1565 to present day)

Beef Wellington brandished the piece of paper at Radish. "If it wasn't for that loathsome busybody, Larkin Lambchop, William Wellington wouldn't have been declared a traitor. AND if William Wellington hadn't been declared a traitor, I'd still be a lord and have tons of money and a big castle."

Radish shook his mane.

"I know, I know, Radish, all William Wellington's riches were seized. But he escaped with the Queen's ruby, remember?" Beef Wellington narrowed his eyes. "If only I knew where to find that jewel, Radish! It's rightfully mine! I shouldn't have to spend the rest of my life polishing boots until they twinkle."

Radish lifted his tail. A steaming pile of manure plopped onto the sawdust.

"I agree with you, Radish," growled Beef Wellington. "It STINKS. The only good thing is that those lousy Lambchops never got hold of the jewel either." He thrust his feet into the polished boots and stood up. He'd come to a decision.

"You know what, Radish?" he said. "Once a Wellington, always a Wellington. Quartermaster Grouch can stuff his snakes and ladders. I'm going to find my ruby. And no one – not even Quartermaster Grouch – is going to stop me." He gathered the rest of his uniform, picked his way carefully through the sawdust, untied Radish and led him out of the stables. Then he jumped on his back.

Radish pricked up his ears. He pawed the ground eagerly.

Beef Wellington's face had set into a determined expression.

Chapter 4

That afternoon on the River Thames...

Ermine sat on the top deck of the boat with Minty and Lady Lambchop, taking snapshots with her Polaroid. The boat was called *The Jolly Jester* and was one of several boats that sailed up and down the Thames, showing tourists the sights.

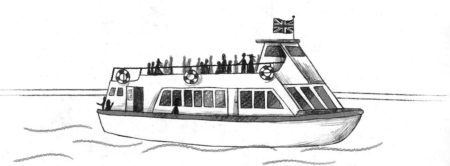

Ermine was still wearing her blue pinafore dress but, on the advice of Minty, had exchanged her waterproof hat for a deerstalker. According to Minty, a famous sleuth called Sherlock Holmes always wore a deerstalker hat and Minty had been very excited to find one on an old doll that was just the right size for Ermine. Ermine was delighted at the thought that it made her look like a real detective, even if it was a bit tickly around the ears.

Ermine wasn't the only one dressed like a detective. Minty was wearing a sunhat and dark glasses (just in case she needed to spy on anyone) and had brought along her Polly Potter Detective Set to decipher clues.

The Jolly Jester puttered gently along the river in the bright sunshine. It had been a very good idea of hers to take the boat, Ermine decided. It was the perfect way to see London!

Now the boat was meandering past the picturesque town of Richmond, on their way to Hampton Court. With its grand houses and green lawns, Ermine thought it was one of the loveliest places she had ever seen.

"In Tudor times, the kings and queens used to travel by barge along the Thames between their palaces," Lady Lambchop told her. "Although London looked very different then!"

Ermine tried to imagine London as it was 450 years ago, without all the tall buildings and cars and red buses and people. She consulted her guidebook to see if there were any pictures. But she spotted something else instead.

She gasped. "Is it true that Henry VIII had *six* wives?" she demanded.

"Yes, it's true!" Minty said. She had just

been learning about the Tudors at school.

"All at the same time?" Ermine asked, aghast.

Minty made a face. "Yuck! No! One after another."

"How come?" asked Ermine.

"Haven't you heard the saying?" Minty replied.

Ermine shook her head. "What saying?"

"Divorced, beheaded, died; divorced, beheaded, survived," said Minty.

DIVORCED: Catherine of Aragon

BEHEADED: Anne Boleyn

DIED: Jane Seymour

DIVORCED: Anne of Cleves

BEHEADED: Catherine Howard

SURVIVED: Catherine Parr

"Beheaded?!" squeaked Ermine.

Minty nodded. "The King got fed up with his first five wives because they didn't give him a son," she explained. "Except the third one, who he loved, but she died. The last one outlived him."

Ermine stroked her whiskers thoughtfully. "Why did Henry VIII want a son so much?" she asked.

"It was tradition," Minty explained. "When the King or Queen of England died, their sons inherited the throne ahead of any daughters."

Ermine looked indignant. "What, even if the boy was a *baby*?" she said.

"That's right," Minty said.

"But you can't be a king if you're a baby!" Ermine spluttered. "You'd be terrible at it.

382

And anyway, it's not fair – girls are just as good at ruling as boys."

"Of course they are," said Minty, "but they didn't think like that then. And Mum was right: in the end the throne *did* pass to Henry VIII's daughter, Elizabeth, and she became a great queen."

"Ha! That proves it then," said Ermine. What silly ideas some humans had about things!

She returned to her guidebook. "Is this her?" Ermine pointed to a picture. It showed a stern lady with a white face and red hair, wearing a splendid dress and a heavy crown encrusted with precious gems.

"Yes, that's her," said Minty. "She's the one who gave the jewel to Larkin Lambchop."

Minty removed her magnifying glass from the **Polly Potter Detective Set**. The two of them used it to study the picture carefully. At the front of the Queen's crown was a big, fat, red ruby. "Ermine! Look!" cried Minty. "I think that might be the Lambchop ruby!"

But something else had caught Ermine's attention. "Wait a minute," she said in a horrified tone, "is that *fur* on the Queen's collar?"

Queen Elizabeth I

Fortunately at that moment they rounded a bend in the river and Hampton Court Palace came into view. It was a magnificent building of soft red brick. On either side of the stone entrance stood two great turrets. Behind them, huge chimneys rose into the sky.

Ermine dropped her guidebook and scampered across the deck of the boat to get a better view. "**Ooh, ooh, ooh!**" she squealed in delight. Now they were actually **at** the palace, she had no trouble imagining what life was like in Tudor times. She felt like Queen Elizabeth I arriving at her royal abode!

The boat docked. Ermine collected her tool bag while Minty shoved the guidebook in her pocket and grabbed the **Detective Set**. The two of them stepped off the gangplank with Lady Lambchop.

"I'll go and explore the gardens while you two investigate," said Lady Lambchop. "See you back here in two hours. Good luck!" She waved goodbye.

Minty pulled her sun hat down over her

ears. "Let's start in the kitchens," she said to Ermine. "And we'd better make sure no one's following us."

"Why would they be?" said Ermine.

"Who knows?" said Minty mysteriously. "But you can never be too careful when you're a detective."

She led the way through the stone entrance and across a cobbled courtyard. Ermine scampered behind. This was their chance to make history!

CLIP CLOP, CLIP CLOP, CLIP CLOP!

The sound of hooves on the stones made Ermine turn her head.

A **HUGE** black horse trotted across the courtyard. On its back rode a soldier, dressed in a scarlet tunic, white jodhpurs and long black boots.

On his head he wore a plumed silver helmet, and tucked into his belt was a long silver sword.

The horse came to a halt. The soldier dismounted and tethered it to a post. "Stay here," he told the horse.

The horse snorted.

"Pssst! Minty!" Ermine hissed.

Minty stopped and turned. "What?"

"Why is there a horse in the courtyard? And who's that man? You don't think *he's* following us, do you?

He does look a little suspicious."

Minty looked at the horse and rider from under her hat. Then she shrugged. "You don't need to worry about *him*, Ermine. He's one of the royal guards. This way!" Minty disappeared through a door.

Ermine followed her into a smaller courtyard crowded with barrels and carts. They entered a building called the Boiling House.

"I don't know about Boiling *House*," grumbled Ermine from under the deerstalker, "but it's boiling *hot*!"

They passed through the Boiling House along a narrow street and into the main kitchens. Ermine couldn't believe how many buildings there were. Hampton Court was more like a village than a palace.

Inside the Great Kitchen it was even hotter. A huge fire roared in the grate, like in Tudor times. To one side of the fireplace a man dressed in Tudor costume slowly turned a haunch of meat on a spit.

Ermine whipped off her deerstalker and

began to fan her ears with it. "Minty! **Look!** That must be where Larkin Lambchop was when he spotted William Wellington poisoning the Queen's pie!" she squealed. She hurried over to where the Tudor man sat.

Minty hurried after her.

"I'm Ermine Stoat," Ermine said importantly, "and this is my assistant, Minty."

"**What?**" cried Minty. "But you're supposed to be *my* assistant!"

Ermine frowned. "I'm the one with the special hat, remember?" She turned back to the man. "We're **detectives**. We're here to solve the mystery of the missing Lambchop ruby."

There was a great clatter behind them.

☀ CRASH! ☀

Ermine and Minty looked around. To Ermine's surprise, the soldier in the red tunic sat in a heap on the floor beside a table, surrounded by fallen pots and pans.

Ermine scurried over and fanned him with her hat. "Are you all right?" she said.

The soldier stared back at her, open-mouthed. He looked as if he'd had a terrible shock.

"He must have fainted from the heat," said Minty. "He needs water."

"Leave it to me." Ermine shimmied up the table leg and grabbed an old stone flask. She pulled the stopper out with her teeth and poured the contents over the soldier's head.

"That's not water – it's mead!" cried the Tudor man.

Ermine didn't know what mead was, but

from its gluey consistency, the sickly smell
and the number of flies buzzing around
the soldier's hair, it was made
from something sweet
and sticky.

"It's a Tudor drink made from honey," Minty whispered.

"Oh," said Ermine. That explained the flies. "Sorry about that," she said to the soldier, while the Tudor man handed him a glass of water and helped him to a chair.

The soldier still seemed in a daze. Minty was right, thought Ermine, the heat must have gotten to him. Either that or he'd seen a ghost. An old place like Hampton Court must be full of them. She returned to the fireplace with Minty and the Tudor man.

"You know all about the Great Pastry Plot then?" said the Tudor man.

Minty and Ermine nodded solemnly. "We intend to find out where Lord Wellington hid the Queen's ruby," said Minty.

"It belongs to Minty's family, you see," explained Ermine. "She's a Lambchop. Her mom's going to write a **Polly Potter** book about it and her dad's going to use the money to save jungle cats. And we're going to make history by finding it."

There was another clatter.

CRASH!

Ermine looked around. Now the soldier had fallen off his chair!

People fussed around him.

What on earth was the matter with him now? wondered Ermine.

"Do *you* know where we can find some clues?" Minty asked the Tudor man.

"Maybe." The Tudor man scratched his beard. "Have you heard the old rhyme?" he said.

Ermine and Minty shook their heads.

"It goes like this," said the Tudor man.

Cock-a-doodle-doo,
a plot began to brew.
Wellington poisoned the pie,
left the Queen to die,
But Lambchop knew what to do.
Concerned for her safety,
He shouted, *"THE PASTRY!"*
But William escaped
down the loo.

Minty wrote it in her Polly Potter notebook. "So that's how he escaped! I didn't even know they *had* loos in those days."

"Me neither," said Ermine. "I thought people went in the woods, like weasels."

"Not at court," said the Tudor man. "Here – I'll show you."

He led the way out of the kitchens and up the stairs to an enormous gallery lined with tapestries. Ermine sat on Minty's shoulder, clutching her tool bag. She gazed in awe at the beautiful wooden ceiling.

"That's where Elizabeth I was sitting

when it happened." The Tudor man pointed to a great throne at the far end of the gallery. "And this is where Wellington made his escape." He led them past the throne into a small room. Inside the room, tucked discreetly into the wall behind a tapestry, was an ancient toilet. Ermine peered down it cautiously, one paw placed delicately over her nose, just in case.

"It's called a garderobe," said the Tudor man. "And don't

worry — it's clean. No one's used it for a few hundred years."

"...re does it come out?" Ermine

"...iver," the Tudor man said.

"...ington climbed down it,

...barge and made his

...probably a bit

...ght have left a clue

...inty wondered.

"There's only one way to find out," said ...mine in a determined voice. "Hold this!"

...e rammed the deerstalker hat into Minty's ...nd. Then she scampered down Minty's ...ralls to the floor, opened her tool bag and ...k out a rope and a head lamp.

"Here!" She tied one end of the rope to Minty's ankle and the other end around her waist using a strong knot, strapped the head lamp firmly around her ears, jumped into the hole and abseiled down the loo.

It all happened so quickly that Minty

worry – it's clean. No one's used it for a few hundred years."

"Where does it come out?" Ermine asked.

"The river," the Tudor man said. "William Wellington climbed down it, jumped on a passing barge and made his getaway. Though he was probably a bit **smelly** by that point."

"Do you think he might have left a clue *in the loo*?" Minty wondered.

"There's only one way to find out," said Ermine in a determined voice. "Hold this!" She rammed the deerstalker hat into Minty's hand. Then she scampered down Minty's overalls to the floor, opened her tool bag and took out a rope and a head lamp.

"Here!" She tied one end of the rope to Minty's ankle and the other end around her waist using a strong knot, strapped the head lamp firmly around her ears, jumped into the hole and abseiled down the loo.

It all happened so quickly that Minty and the Tudor man barely had time to blink!

Minty leaned over the shaft. She cupped her hands around her mouth so she could shout down.

"ARE YOU OKAY, ERMINE?"

"OF COURSE I'M OKAY!" came a squeaky echo from somewhere far below. "I THINK I'VE FOUND SOMETHING! WAIT, I'LL TAKE A PHOTO."

POOF!

Ermine's camera flashed.

POOF!

It flashed again.

There was a tug on the rope. "PULL ME UP!" Ermine ordered.

Minty placed both hands on the rope and pulled.

After a moment, Ermine came into view. She leaped out of the hole straight into Minty's pocket.

"Can I see the pictures?" Minty said.

"Not here," whispered Ermine. "They're top secret. And it was you who said there might be someone following us, remember!" She looked about furtively. "Let's go somewhere private and I'll show you. Can you think of anywhere?"

Minty's eyes lit up. "How about the maze?" she said.

Chapter 5

A little while later,
at the Hampton Court maze...

Corporal Beef Wellington hid behind a large stone statue near the entrance of the maze. Radish stood beside him, pulling clumps of lush grass from the lawn with his big teeth and chewing them noisily.

CHOMP, CHOMP, CHOMP!

"I'm telling you, Radish, it could talk!" Beef Wellington swiped at a bee. His hair was still sticky from the mead and his red tunic was stained an unpleasant treacly brown.

Radish snorted.

"It *could,* Radish! It's a stoat detective. It's got a deerstalker hat and a magnifying glass. The Lambchops must have hired it to uncover the mystery of what happened to the Queen's ruby." He swiped at another bee.

Radish tore off an even bigger clump of grass and chewed that too. Galloping all the way from the barracks to Hampton Court was hungry work for a big horse.

CHOMP, CHOMP, CHOMP!

Beef Wellington elbowed his steed in the ribs. "Will you stop stuffing your face and listen to me, Radish? It's a detective. A particularly sneaky one, if you ask me. And it's after MY treasure. It found a CLUE in the loo!" He swiped at a third bee. The beastly things were everywhere.

Radish's head jerked up. The horse looked at its owner questioningly.

"Yes, *that* loo – the one William Wellington escaped down in 1565," said Beef Wellington. "The stoat abseiled down it and took a photo of something. And before you ask how I know, I was hiding behind the tapestry outside the garderobe.

"That's why we're here. So we can spy on it again – it might lead us to the ruby." He pulled Radish's reins.

"*Shhh!* Look, there it is! Over there with the girl."

Ermine and Minty were approaching the maze. Ermine had resumed her place on Minty's shoulder, her deerstalker hat pulled down firmly over her ears.

"Two tickets, please," Ermine said to the attendant in a loud, clear voice.

"*See?*" Beef Wellington hissed. Radish clacked his teeth in astonishment.

"Can I interest you in a joint ticket for the apiary?" the attendant asked Ermine.

"What's that?" asked Ermine.

"The royal beehives," said the attendant.

"They're just over there." He pointed to a group of small wooden huts tucked away under some trees.

"Is that where you get the honey for the mead?" asked Ermine with interest. "I just spilled some by accident in the kitchen."

"That's right," said the attendant. He chuckled and lowered his voice. "But don't tell the bees!" he whispered. "They don't much like having their honey taken."

"I don't blame them," Ermine whispered back. "We stoats don't much like having our fur taken."

Beef Wellington strained to hear. *What were they whispering about? Was it something to do with bees?*

"I'll let you into a little secret," murmured

the attendant. "There's only one thing bees hate more than having their honey taken – and that's something eating their foxgloves."

Beef Wellington couldn't quite catch it. *Foxes? What did foxes have to do with bees?* He shook his head crossly. He wished they'd speak up.

"Thanks for the tip," said Minty in a normal voice. "We'll just do the maze today."

The attendant handed her the tickets. "Don't get lost!" he said cheerily.

"Don't worry, stoats have an excellent sense of direction!" Ermine replied.

"They're ermazing at mazes," Minty giggled.

The two of them disappeared inside amid peals of laughter.

"Come on, Radish," Beef Wellington hissed,

swatting at another bee. He took hold of the horse's bridle. "We'll go the other way. Then we can spy on them when they get to the middle." He and Radish waited until the attendant's back was turned and tiptoed through the exit gate.

Beef and Radish hurried along the narrow passage between the tall hedges until they came to a fork in the path.

"This way!" Beef Wellington said, leading Radish to the left.

On they went between the tall hedges until they came to another fork in the path.

"This way!" Beef Wellington said, leading Radish to the right.

On they went again.

"Curses!" said Beef Wellington. They'd reached a dead end. "Have a look and see where we are, will you, Radish?"

Radish reared up on his hind legs and peeked over the hedge, only to see Ermine and Minty hurrying by in the opposite direction.

He waved a hoof to show his owner which way they'd gone.

"Back, back!" said Beef Wellington. He felt very hot and flustered. The syrupy mead was sticking to him like glue. It was all that meddling stoat's fault! Beef Wellington had a good mind to let Radish trample it. More and more bees buzzed around his ears and tunic.

They got to a fork in the path. "This way!" Beef Wellington said, leading Radish to the right.

On they went between the hedges until they came to another fork in the path.

"This way!" Beef Wellington said, leading Radish to the left.

On they went again.

"Curses!" said Beef Wellington. They were back where they'd started!

BZZZZZZZZZZZZZZ...
ZZZZZZZZZZZZZ ...
BZZZZZZZZZZ!

And the bothersome bees were gathering
in number. They seemed to be attracted to
the mead.

"We'll just have to cheat," Beef Wellington
said crossly. He leaped on to Radish's back
and bent low in the saddle like a racing jockey.

"Tally-ho, Radish!"

Radish cantered along the path between the hedges, closely pursued by the bees. This time, whenever they reached a dead end, instead of trying to find another way around, Radish jumped over it.

A few jumps later, Beef Wellington drew the horse to a halt. He could hear voices. They were almost at the middle of the maze!

Beef Wellington peered
cautiously over the hedge.
Minty and Ermine sat on a bench
in a small clearing surrounded by tall
foxgloves. The two of them were poring
over a Polaroid picture with
Minty's magnifying glass.

The clue in the loo!

Ha ha! Beef Wellington smiled to himself. Stoats and Lambchops weren't the only ones who could play detective! It was his family treasure, and he was going to be the one to find it! He took out a small brass telescope from his tunic pocket. The telescope was a family heirloom – one of the few things passed down through generations of the Wellington family after they were stripped of their wealth. He put the telescope to his eye and twisted the barrel until the photograph came into focus.

Beef Wellington found himself squinting at a picture of what looked very much like ancient graffiti. He gasped. William Wellington the Traitor must have scrawled it on the garderobe during his escape so that his family would be able to find the jewel if he was ever caught!

Beef Wellington read it carefully. Or at least he tried to.

The ruby is mine. None shall know.
Now on to the Archbishop's Garden I go.

(Lord) William Wellington 1865

Beef Wellington scratched his head. It didn't make any sense!

Just then Minty carefully removed something from a slim briefcase and handed it to Ermine. Beef Wellington zoomed in with the telescope to get a better look.

He barely had time to register that the object in Ermine's paws was a compact mirror when she opened it.

BOOF!

The sun's rays reflected
off the mirror onto the
telescope lens, down the
barrel and straight into
Beef Wellington's eye.
The glare was so bright
it nearly made him
fall off Radish.

Beef Wellington clutched his head in agony. His temples throbbed. He could feel his headache worsening.

Painfully he steadied himself and forced his eyes open to take another look.

Now Ermine was holding the photograph up to the mirror, while Minty jotted something down in a notebook.

Beef Wellington frowned. What on earth were they doing?

Suddenly the penny dropped. The clue in the loo was in mirror writing! The letters were reversed. If you saw it in a mirror, you could read it.

He raised the telescope cautiously and zoomed in on the notebook.

419

The ruby is mine. None shall know.
Now on to the Archbishop's Garden I go.

(Lord) William Wellington 1565

A wicked smile spread across Beef Wellington's face. *The Archbishop's Garden.* He knew exactly where that was!

He pocketed the telescope and ducked down behind the hedge. Ermine and Minty were getting ready to go, but Beef wasn't worried about them any more. He had this treasure hunt in the bag! All he had to do was make sure he got to the ruby before they did.

He waited until they'd disappeared, then dug his heels into Radish's flanks. "*Tally-ho, Radish!*" he hissed.

But Radish didn't budge. Instead, Beef

Wellington felt a strong tug on the reins.

YANK!

While Beef Wellington had been spying

on Minty and Ermine, Radish had been

doing some spying of his own.

FOXGLOVES!

Radish stretched his powerful neck over

the hedge and lunged at the luscious flowers.

He tore off a big clump and began to chew.

CHOMP CHOMP CHOMP.

Then he tore off another big clump

and chewed that too.

CHOMP CHOMP CHOMP.

Beef Wellington looked

around in alarm. An angry

buzzing was coming from

close behind them.

BZZZZZZZZZ!
BZZZZZZZZ!

The bees!

But the bees weren't just bothersome any more. They were positively **scary**. A great cloud of them had formed above Radish's tail. Beef Wellington gulped.

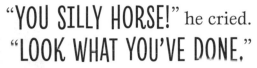

"YOU SILLY HORSE!" he cried.
"LOOK WHAT YOU'VE DONE,"

Radish stopped
mid-chomp. He
swished his tail
angrily at the bees.

BZZZZZZZZZZ!
BZZZZZZZZZZZZZZZZZ!

The bees ignored
him. One of them flew down
and stung Radish hard on his rump.
Radish let out a squeal. He bucked and reared.
Beef Wellington clung to the saddle.
"STOP IT, RADISH!" he shouted.

But Radish wasn't
listening. All of a sudden, he bolted.

Ermine and Minty had reached the
exit of the maze.

"LOOK OUT!" cried Minty.

The two of them crouched down as a large
black horse bearing the red-
coated cavalry soldier
sailed over their heads
and thundered across
the gardens towards
the River Thames,

closely pursued by a
swarm of bees.

There was a loud

SPLASH.

"**Oh dear,**" said Ermine. "I hope
they can swim."

Chapter 6

The next morning at 17 Mutton Lane

Ermine and Minty sat at the breakfast table in their pajamas, surrounded by Lord Lambchop's cats and puzzling over the clue in the loo. Minty's pajamas were covered in cats, like the kitchen. Ermine's were an eye-catching shade of pink.

> The ruby is mine. None shall know.
> Now on to the Archbishop's Garden I go.

Ermine's London guidebook was propped up against the teapot. She leafed through it briskly while Minty looked up *Archbishop's Garden* on Lady Lambchop's tablet.

"We're looking for *Tudor* gardens, remember?" Minty said, helping herself to some cereal.

Ermine nodded sagely. She'd already gone through the guidebook and flagged all the Tudor landmarks with sticky notes, on Minty's instructions.

She dunked a toast soldier in her boiled egg, and turned to the next page. "Ooh, ooh, ooh!" she squeaked through a mouthful of eggy toast. "This must be it!"

LAMBETH PALACE and GARDENS

Lambeth Palace was built in 1435. It is the London residence of the Archbishop of Canterbury.

"Brilliant!" said Minty. She put her spoon down and typed the name into the tablet. "Here it is." She clicked on a website.

Ermine dabbed egg yolk off her whiskers with a napkin. "It says in the guidebook it's closed to the public," she said disappointedly.

"Not today it isn't," Minty said as she scrolled down. "Look!" She turned the tablet screen so that Ermine could see.

Lambeth Palace Garden — EVENTS

Lambeth
PALACE
GARDENS
FETE

SATURDAY 30TH JULY
LAMBETH PALACE GARDENS
12.30 P.M. TO 5 P.M.
including

FACE PAINTING   DOG SHOW
LIVE MUSIC   TOMBOLA
STALLS   TUG OF WAR
CREAM TEAS   RAFFLE

"I'll ask Mum if we can go."

Ermine clapped her paws in excitement. *A garden fete!* She'd never been to one before, but the Duchess had told her they were so popular in Britain that even the Queen had one every summer. Ermine couldn't wait to taste the cream tea and try her paw at the tombola. Suddenly a thought struck her. "Minty, is the Archbishop very important?" she asked.

"Of course he is," said Minty. "He's the head of the Church of England."

Ermine snapped the guidebook shut. "Then I shall need to wear my feathered hat," she said.

This time, instead of taking the boat, Lady Lambchop, Minty and Ermine traveled to their destination on the Tube. Ermine didn't like the Tube nearly as much – it was very noisy, packed with people and far too squashy, but she had to admit it was a lot quicker.

Very soon they arrived
at Lambeth. The palace
looked like a mini version
of Hampton Court. The
fete was being held in
the gardens.

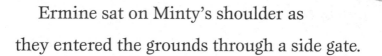

Ermine sat on Minty's shoulder as
they entered the grounds through a side gate.

"Family ticket with free entry to the raffle?"
the lady in the entrance booth asked.

"I'm not really family," Ermine said a
little sadly.

"Of course you are!" the lady replied
cheerfully. "We're ALL part of a family in
Lambeth. We like to think of ourselves as one
big community."

That made Ermine feel so warm and happy

inside she had to stop and take
photos with everyone to put in her
scrapbook to show the Duchess, including
ones with the Lambeth schools jazz band
and the Kennington Tandoori tug-of-war
team, who arrived at
the same time.

"I'm going to the book stall," said Lady Lambchop. "Remember to keep your eyes open for clues!" She waved goodbye.

"Let's make a note of our observations," said Ermine to Minty.

"Good idea," Minty agreed.

Ermine perched on Minty's shoulder while Minty went to work with her notebook and pencil.

The first thing they saw was the ice-cream van.

Ice Cream

★ Ice Cream ★
Van

The second
thing they saw
was the dogs
and their owners
practicing for the
dog show.

The third thing they saw was the soldier
and horse they'd seen at Hampton Court.
Traces of dried mud lingered on the soldier's
boots, and the horse had a big lump on its

rump. It gave Ermine
a dirty look,
as if it wanted
to eat her
feathered hat.

Ermine jammed the hat firmly onto her head. "What's *he* doing here?" she whispered to Minty. "It seems very suspicious that he keeps turning up everywhere."

"I've told you, Ermine, you don't need to worry about him," said Minty. "He's probably guarding the Archbishop or something. Besides, if he was spying on us, he'd be incognito."

"In *what*?" asked Ermine.

"Incognito! It means he'd conceal his identity. Let's go."

Ermine looked at the horse again. Now it seemed to be sneering at her. Its lips were going all wobbly. She frowned. The soldier and his horse might not be spying on them, but there was definitely something funny going on.

They climbed some steps up to a gravel walkway. On the other side of the walkway more steps led down to a wide lawn crowded with stalls and people. Children chased each other in circles around the grass.

"What's that?" Ermine said, pointing to a stone plinth beneath an arch of roses further along the walkway. The plinth looked very old, as if it had been there since at *least* Tudor times.

"It's a sundial," said Minty, going over to look at it.

Ermine was mystified. "What's a sundial?" she asked.

"It's an ancient way of telling the time," said Minty, who'd learned about sundials at school. She placed Ermine on the sundial so she could see better.

The dial was like a clock face with Roman numerals, the number twelve at the top.

"The lines and numbers represent each hour of the day," Minty explained to Ermine. "When the sun shines, you can tell the time from where the triangle's shadow falls."

Ermine was fascinated. "That's really clever!" she said. Then she frowned. "What happens if it's cloudy?"

"I don't know," Minty admitted.

"Do you think the sundial might be a clue?" asked Ermine.

"Maybe," said Minty. She took out her magnifying glass from her **Polly Potter Detective Set** and examined the dial. "Wait a minute," she said. "Look at this."

In the middle of the sundial, just beneath the triangle, someone had scratched a message in tiny letters:

8, 1, 2, 2, 5, 10
WW woz here!
1565

"The sundial must be a decoder ring!" said Minty.

"What's a decoder ring?" Ermine asked. It sounded very mysterious.

"It's a way of sending secret messages," Minty told her. "I've got one in my Detective Set." She took it out and showed it to Ermine.

"Each number represents a letter," Minty explained.

"All we have to do is work out which letters match the numbers, then we've cracked the clue."

"You mean the numbers spell a *word*?" Ermine squeaked. This detective stuff was **thrilling.**

"Precisely," said Minty.

Ermine clapped her paws together. **"Ooh, ooh, ooh!** I **LOVE** puzzles! I do them all the time in Balaclavia with the Duchess!"

Minty began to sketch the dial in her notebook. "I don't get it," she said after a while. "The alphabet has twenty-six letters but the sundial only has twelve numbers. How are we supposed to work out which one represents what?"

"*Shhh!*" said Ermine. "I'm thinking."

She counted something on her toes. "Wait! I think I know! The numbers on the dial go up and down from 12. Maybe the letters do the same." She plucked the pen from Minty's grasp and jotted them down in the notebook.

"So what does it say?" asked Minty breathlessly.

Ermine copied the secret message into the notebook:

8, 1, 2, 2, 5, 10

Then she wrote the matching letters underneath:

W, A, B, B, E, Y

"Wabbey?" said Minty. "What's a wabbey?"

The two of them exchanged mystified glances.

"Wait! I think I know!" said Ermine. She pulled out her London guidebook from Minty's pocket and opened it to a yellow sticky note.

It was one of the places she'd looked up that morning.

"Westminster Abbey!" exclaimed Minty. "Of course! Ermine, you're a GENIUS!"

"Well, maybe *not* a genius…" began Ermine modestly.

Just then a voice came over the loud speaker:

WOULD MISS ERMINE STOAT PLEASE REPORT TO THE RAFFLE TENT WHERE THE ARCHBISHOP IS WAITING TO PRESENT HER PRIZE.

"Woohoo, Ermine!" cried Minty. "You won a **prize!** Let's go and get it. Then we can play Splat the Rat." She snapped her notebook shut.

Ermine straightened her feathered hat. This really was turning out to be the

BEST DAY <u>EVER!</u>

Chapter 7

The next day at the barracks...

Beef Wellington was having a HORRIBLE morning.

5 a.m. parade practice was pathetic...
6 a.m. breakfast was beastly...
7 a.m. mucking out was manky...
And 8 a.m. running was rotten.

Now he was back in the stables, polishing Radish's hooves. It seemed like everything was going wrong. The mead. The bees. The river. And to top it all, Lambeth Palace was only open to the public one day a year. He'd had to go along to the garden fete just like everyone else. And guess who'd arrived just ahead of him…

"I **HATE** that smarty-pants **weasel detective** and her little friend," said Beef Wellington bitterly.

Radish snorted in agreement.

"I mean, it's bad enough them going after **my** treasure, but winning a raffle prize as well – that's just plain unfair."

Beef Wellington had never won a raffle prize in his life, let alone met an archbishop. In fact, he'd never won anything – not even an egg-and-spoon race. He ground his teeth at the injustice of it all. "Well, one thing's for sure, Radish – that weasel's <u>not</u> getting its paws on the Wellington ruby." He stood up and gave Radish a sugar lump. "Luckily I had my telescope with me," he grumbled, "although they've even managed to ruin *that*!"

Beef Wellington withdrew the telescope from his tunic and regarded it crossly. He'd tried to sneak up on Minty and Ermine at the fete, with the result that the telescope had been crushed by Minty's wonky aim with the hammer at the Splat the Rat game.

It looked more like a periscope than a telescope now. But it *had* come in handy for spying around corners when Minty and Ermine were watching the dog show…

"Westminster Abbey," he said thoughtfully. "I wonder if the treasure's actually *hidden* there, or if there's another clue…" He scratched Radish fondly between the ears. "Well, we'll soon find out, Radish. Once we escape from Quartermaster Grouch…"

The stable door banged.

"It's him!" Beef Wellington hissed. "Leave it to me, Radish. I'll do the talking."

Quartermaster Grouch marched over.

LEFT. RIGHT. LEFT. RIGHT.

LEFT. RIGHT.

"WHAT COLOR DO YOU CALL THOSE, WELLINGTON?" he shouted, pointing at the mud-stained boots.

"Green, sir," said Beef Wellington. "GREEN?????!!!!!" yelled the Quartermaster. "THEY SHOULD BE TWINKLING LIKE STARS, <u>NOT</u> GREEN LIKE WELLINGTONS, WELLINGTON!"

"Yes, sir."

"AND WHAT'S *THAT* ON YOUR TUNIC?" Quartermaster Grouch demanded, eyeing the brown patches with disgust.

"It's mead, sir."

"MEAD?????" Quartermaster Grouch roared.

Beef Wellington nodded.

"THIS ISN'T A TUDOR PICNIC, WELLINGTON!"

450

shouted the Quartermaster.

"No, sir!"

"YOU'RE **NOT** HENRY VIII."

"Definitely not, sir."

"YOU'RE A MEMBER OF THE HOUSEHOLD CAVALRY, WELLINGTON. YOU SHOULDN'T BE DRINKING MEAD."

"I *didn't* drink it, sir," said Beef Wellington. "A talking weasel poured it over my head in the kitchens at Hampton Court Palace."

The Quartermaster looked as if he might explode.

A TALKING WEASEL???!!! THAT PROVES IT, WELLINGTON. YOU'RE LOONY! GO AND HAVE A COLD BATH...

(Having a cold bath was another one of the Quartermaster's cruel and unusual punishments.)

"AND TAKE YOUR HORSE WITH YOU.

IT'S GOT A **LUMP** ON ITS **RUMP**
THE SIZE OF A **CAMEL'S HUMP!**"

"Yes, sir," said Beef Wellington meekly.

"AND NO **JAMMIE DODGERS**
FOR A **WEEK!**" (That was another.)

Quartermaster Grouch marched out of the stables.

LEFT. RIGHT. LEFT. RIGHT.
LEFT. RIGHT.

Beef Wellington leaped off the stool.

He had no intention of having a cold bath,

especially not with Radish.

"Tally-ho, Radish," he said. "Next stop
– Westminster Abbey! We need to get there
before that repulsive weasel and her Lambchop
friend, so we can find the next clue before they
do and get back the Wellington jewel."

453

They cantered out
of the barracks...

past Buckingham Palace...

through St. James's Park...

and into
Parliament Square.

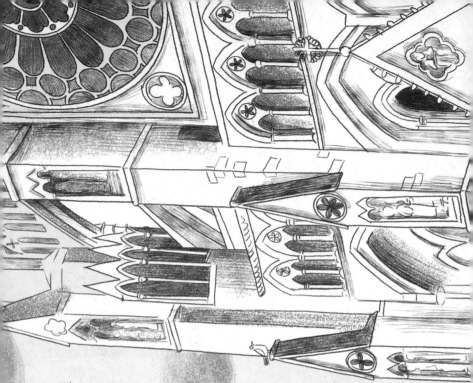

A few minutes later they arrived outside Westminster Abbey – just in time to see the great wooden doors open and Minty and Ermine disappear inside.

"**CURSES!**" cried Beef Wellington. "They're here already!" He quickly dismounted.

"Wait here, Radish."

Radish shook his head and pawed at the ground.

Beef Wellington relented. "Oh all right, Radish, you can come with me. But if anyone sees you, freeze. They'll think you're a statue. You got that?"

Radish whinnied.

They crept through the great door.

"Look! There they are!" hissed Beef Wellington.

Ermine and Minty had joined a tour group. The two of them were listening avidly to the guide.

Radish shook his mane at seeing Ermine again. His rump was still *very* sore.

"Come on, Radish – the guide might have some clues!"

Beef Wellington and Radish hurried along the aisle, keeping to the side. Luckily for them, the abbey was so echoey that no one noticed the sound of Radish's hooves CLIP-CLOPPING on the tiled floor.

They stopped a little way away from the group. Beef Wellington listened closely.

"Most visitors enter the Abbey through the

north transept," said the guide. "Their first
impression is of the soaring height of the vaulted
ceiling. At 102 feet, it is the highest in England."

The group looked up in awe, including
Ermine, who was sitting on Minty's shoulder,
wearing her detective hat and taking notes in
her scrapbook.

"Get on with it!" muttered Beef Wellington. He couldn't care less about the vaulted ceiling. Wellingtons weren't known for their climbing – he was sure there wouldn't be any clues up there.

"The rose window above the entrance is one of the finest stained-glass windows in the world," said the guide.

Everyone looked.

No clues there either, thought Beef Wellington fretfully, chewing his fingernails.

"The north transept also contains several larger-than-life statues of early prime ministers…"

Beef Wellington suddenly realized that the guide was pointing towards him and Radish.

"Freeze, Radish!" he hissed, ducking down in the nick of time behind an early prime minister.

Radish froze.

460

"And...er...one of their horses,"
said the guide.

The group moved off.

Once they were sure no one was looking, Beef Wellington and Radish hurried along the aisle to catch up with them. This time they hid behind a coffin.

"Thirty-nine monarchs have been crowned in Westminster Abbey," said the guide. "They have all been crowned sitting in the Coronation Chair."

"Was Elizabeth I crowned in the Coronation Chair?" Minty asked.

"Yes." The guide nodded.

"It's a bit scruffy," observed Ermine doubtfully. The Coronation Chair wasn't nearly as grand as she had expected. It was more like the sort of thing you'd find at a garage sale.

Beef Wellington tried to get a look
with his telescope.

He could see what she meant. The chair
was covered in graffiti.

"Most of the graffiti was carved many years ago by pupils from nearby Westminster School," explained the guide. "They used to sneak into the Abbey during the night and leave messages."

"What about the rest of the messages?" Minty asked. "Is there anything about treasure?"

"Well, there's this one," said the guide. He pointed at one of the carvings.

Beef Wellington and Radish exchanged feverish glances.

Ermine and Minty squinted at the chair. Then Minty opened the Polly Potter Detective Set and took out a piece of tracing paper and a pencil. She held the paper against the carving while Ermine got to work.

"They're making a rubbing, Radish!"

464

whispered Beef Wellington. "It must be a clue!"

He zoomed in with the telescope.

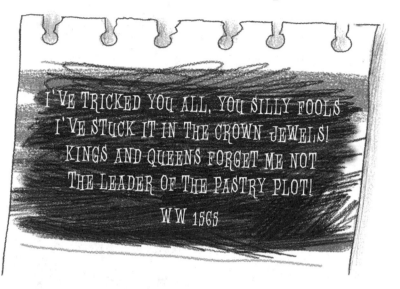

Beef Wellington blinked. *Of course!*

The Crown Jewels!

No wonder the Wellington treasure had remained hidden for so long. What better place to hide the Queen's ruby than with other royal gems?

The Tower of London. It was the last place anyone would think to look!

Beef Wellington's face broke into a joyful grin. If they hurried, he and Radish would be there before the Lambchop girl and the weasel. Nothing could stop him now! The ruby was almost in his grasp. William Wellington would be proud of him.

Just imagine, thought Beef dreamily as he tiptoed out of the Abbey with Radish, *if the Great Pastry Plot had actually succeeded.* William Wellington would have become King of England. He'd have had all the jewels he wanted – not just one ruby…

Suddenly Beef had a brainwave. The thought of his devious ancestor had given him the most **fantastic idea**. *Why not steal all the Crown Jewels while he was there?* They practically belonged to him anyway. Or they should. He, Beef, might not become king (well, not yet, anyway) but he could still be richer than any Wellington had ever been! He could buy an island, or five, and live there with Radish for the rest of his life in a big castle. They would eat caviar and sugar lumps and watch movies all day, while sharks swam around the moat, keeping out weasels.

And he would never have to see small, furry, brown detectives, Lambchops or Quartermaster Grouch EVER again.

Beef Wellington gave an evil chuckle. Talk about history. It was time to go out all buns blazing. The Great Pastry Plot was about to rise again. He leaped onto his horse's back.

"Tally-ho, Radish! To the Tower!"

They galloped off in the direction of the Tower of London.

Chapter 8

Closing time at the Tower of London...

Ermine and Minty had also worked out the clue.

"So **that's** where the ruby is!" said Lady Lambchop as they jumped in a black taxi. "No wonder no one has ever found it until now!"

"I should have realized!" said Minty. "It's called hiding in plain sight – when you hide something somewhere so obvious that no one thinks to look there."

Hiding in plain sight. Ermine made a mental note of it for the future. It was clearly something all good detectives should know.

Very soon they had arrived at the Tower of London.

The Tower was the most imposing of all the Tudor landmarks Ermine had yet seen. The massive stone turrets loomed high above her as dark storm clouds gathered in the sky.

They hurried across the moat to the portcullis. A man stepped out from behind the iron grille. He was dressed in a bright-red uniform: red stockings, a frilly collar and a broad-brimmed hat adorned with fluffy bobbles. In one arm he carried a vicious-looking pike.

"Who's *he?*" Ermine whispered to Minty in alarm. "He's a Yeoman of the Guard," Minty told her. "They're also called **beefeaters.**"

How odd, thought Ermine. But then most things about London were a little bit odd. It must have to do with its history – a history that Ermine still very much intended to be a part of!

"HALT! Who goes there?" said the beefeater.

Ermine took charge. "I do," she said. "And so does my friend Minty, and her mother, Lady Lambchop."

"Lambchop, you say?" said the beefeater. "As in LARKIN LAMBCHOP?"

Ermine nodded. "We've been investigating the mystery of the Great Pastry Plot—" she began.

"We know where William Wellington put the Lambchop treasure—" Minty interrupted.

"It's hidden in the Crown Jewels," Ermine interrupted back. She wished Minty would behave more like a sidekick sometimes. She really would have to have a word with her about it if they were ever to solve any more mysteries together.

The beefeater whistled. "You'd better come in." He raised the portcullis. "My name's Greville, by the way."

Just then hooves pounded on the cobbles. They turned around.

A great black horse with a lump on its rump the size of a camel's hump galloped across the drawbridge towards them. On its back was a soldier dressed in a stained red tunic and dirty boots. He was brandishing a wonky telescope and had a crazy look in his eye.

"TALLY-HO, RADISH!" he yelled.
"WATCH OUT!" cried the beefeater.
Everyone scattered just in time.

The horse gave a loud snort. It made a horrible face at Ermine as it shot past.

"Them again!" said Ermine. She turned to Minty. "Who do you think he's guarding *this* time, Minty? Only, I think they might be following us."

"He's not guarding anyone," confirmed the beefeater. "That's been the beefeaters' job at the Tower since Tudor times."

"So what's he *really* doing here?" said Minty.

"I don't know," said Ermine. "But something tells me we'd better find out."

The little group chased after the horse and rider.

"LET'S TAKE THE SHORTCUT!" shouted the beefeater, diving left under a low archway.

The Tower was a bit like Hampton Court, Ermine realized. Inside it were streets, buildings and grassy squares, most of which seemed to have very gruesome names. Ermine caught sight of two of them as they

rushed along, which was enough to tell her that she didn't want to see any more.

There was also a pen containing some large black birds with vicious-looking beaks.

She hurried past with a shiver.

In a little while they arrived outside the Jewel House.

Ermine gazed up at it. The Jewel House was like a castle all by itself. It had thick, stone walls and a pair of big black gates, with the words

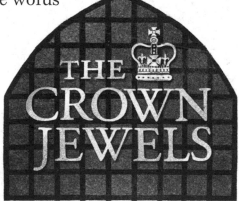

written above them in huge gold letters. One of the gates was open.

From inside the Jewel House there came a SMASH, followed by the shrill scream of a burglar alarm.

BRRRRRRRRRRRRRRRRR!

"I had a feeling that man was up to no good!" said Ermine.

"HE'S STEALING THE CROWN JEWELS!" cried Minty.

"We've got to stop him!" said Ermine in a determined voice. "Come on!"

"I'LL CALL FOR HELP!" cried the beefeater. He and Lady Lambchop raced off.

Minty and Ermine crept into the Jewel House. The heavy metal door guarding the vault where the Crown Jewels were kept was open. They peered around it. Inside the vault they could see a walkway lined with glass cabinets full of precious treasure.

SMASH! CRASH!

Ermine gasped. The soldier and his horse were working their way along the cabinets. The horse was **smashing** each glass panel with a well-aimed kick of its powerful back legs. The soldier followed after it, pulling things out of the cabinets and stuffing them into a nosebag.

"*What are we going to do?*" whispered Minty in dismay.

Ermine cast her eyes along the display cabinets. At the very end was one containing a mannequin of Elizabeth I. The mannequin was clothed in a **magnificent** velvet dress. In one hand it held a scepter, in the other hand an orb. And on its head was a crown encrusted with jewels – the most gorgeous of which was a glittering, red ruby.

She gave Minty's hair a tug. "Minty, look! That's IT! The LAMBCHOP RUBY!"

CLANK! CRASH! THUMP!

The soldier and his horse made their way towards it, throwing things into the nosebag.

The soldier was muttering William Wellington's final message under his breath:

"I'VE TRICKED YOU ALL, YOU SILLY FOOLS
I'VE STUCK IT IN THE CROWN JEWELS!
KINGS AND QUEENS FORGET ME NOT
THE LEADER OF THE PASTRY PLOT!"

"He's gone **mad!**" whispered Minty.

It was true, thought Ermine. The soldier had a reckless look about him. Not to mention his dirty appearance. That dip in the river at Hampton Court hadn't done the trick – he looked as if his uniform needed a good wash.

Suddenly she had a **brilliant idea**. "Minty, do you still have that prize I won at the garden fete?" she whispered.

Minty nodded. "It's in my backpack. Why?"

Ermine whispered something else, very quietly, in Minty's ear.

Minty's face lit up. "Great thinking," she hissed. "I'm in!" She high-fived Ermine's outstretched paw.

Ermine collected her TOOL BAG from Minty's pocket and set off at a run. She scampered along the floor to the back of the last display cabinet.

Quick as a flash, she opened the **TOOL BAG** and removed a hairpin and four tiny suction pads.

Taking the hairpin in her mouth, she placed a pad in each of her paws and **squirmed** up the glass to the lock. Ermine inserted the pin. She twiddled it carefully with her teeth.

CLICK!

It only took a few seconds for the lock to give.

Ermine let go of the suction pads and dropped to the base of the cabinet. Then she pulled open the glass door as far as she could so that Radish wouldn't kick it. Finally she **scurried** up the back of the mannequin's magnificent dress and draped herself across the neckline, in a **perfect** imitation of an ermine collar. *Whew!* she thought to herself. *Just in time! This hiding-in-plain-sight thing had better work!*

Beef Wellington and Radish were approaching. **"HA HA, RADISH!"** cried Beef Wellington.

"HERE IT IS AT LAST! THE WELLINGTON FAMILY JEWEL!"

He reached forward and plucked the ruby from the crown.

"NOT SO FAST!" cried Ermine, uncurling herself from the mannequin's neck.

Beef Wellington and Radish boggled at her. They both looked terrified, as if they thought the mannequin might suddenly come to life too!

Seizing her chance, Ermine sprang forwards, snatching the ruby from the astonished soldier's grasp.

Clasping the jewel in her teeth, Ermine raced back towards the exit.

Radish gave an angry neigh.

Beef Wellington recovered himself.

"IT'S THAT PESTILENT WEASEL DETECTIVE AGAIN!" he shouted, mounting the horse. **"QUICK, RADISH! AFTER IT! WE WELLINGTONS DON'T GIVE UP THAT EASILY."**

So that's it! thought Ermine as she scampered along. *The soldier is a descendent of William Wellington.* No wonder he'd been following them. He'd been trying to work out the clues so he could find the ruby his ancestor had hidden!

She dashed towards the door of the vault.

"DON'T WORRY, ERMINE, I'VE GOT THEM COVERED!" Minty shouted. **"NO ONE GETS PAST MINTY LAMBCHOP, ESPECIALLY <u>NOT</u> A WELLINGTON."** She reached into her backpack and took out Ermine's raffle prize.

BUBBLICIOUS – THE WORLD'S BUBBLIEST BUBBLE BATH

Minty opened the door of the vault.

Ermine shot through onto the cobbles. Outside it had finally started to pour with rain.

Radish galloped after her, a diamond tiara attached rakishly to his ears.

The nosebag swung from his bridle, jingling with swag.

"Get that weasel, Radish!" snarled Beef Wellington from the saddle.

Ermine stopped dead in her tracks. She removed the ruby from her teeth and turned to face them.

"I am <u>not</u> a weasel, I'm a STOAT!" she cried haughtily. "And you shouldn't be stealing other people's treasure! Minty – let them have it!"

Ermine leaped out of the way.

Minty squeezed the bubble-bath bottle as hard as she could.

Its **bubblicious** contents squirted in a great arc onto the rain-soaked cobbles.

Radish's hooves slithered and slid.

Beef Wellington tried to pull him up, but it was no good. The courtyard was as slippery as an ice rink! Horse and rider skated rapidly across it.

CRASH!

Beef Wellington and Radish crashed into a pile of old trash bags.

CLONK!

The swag bag fell at Minty's feet.

ZIP!

The tiara flew off Radish's ears and landed on Ermine's head.

Minty rushed over to where Ermine
still stood holding the dazzling ruby.
"WE DID IT, ERMINE!" she cried,
scooping Ermine up and giving her a
HUGE hug. "HOORAY!"

Beef Wellington pulled a banana skin off his head. "I'll get you for this!" he snarled.

The sound of sirens came from nearby. The police were on their way.

"No you won't," said Minty. "You'll end up in prison where you belong, like your ancestor William."

"Whereas Minty and I will go down in history as the BRILLIANT detectives who solved the mystery of the missing Lambchop treasure," said Ermine happily.

Radish bared his teeth.

Ermine paid no attention. She'd had enough of Radish and his funny faces. Instead she retrieved her Polaroid from Minty's backpack and pointed it at where the bad guys lay in a smelly heap.

"Do you mind if Minty takes a photo for my scrapbook?" she said. "The Duchess did say I had to fill it up!"

Dear Duchess,

Minty and I have been learning all about the Tudors. We've visited lots of palaces and I've met some very interesting people, including the Archbishop of Canterbury, the children from the Lambeth schools jazz band and the Kennington Tandoori tug-of-war team, not to mention Greville the beefeater. We also managed to solve the mystery of the Great Pastry Plot and recover the long-lost Lambchop ruby. It turned out Lord William Wellington hid it in the Crown Jewels! (Great detectives like Minty and I call that hiding something in plain sight, which is what I did by pretending to be an ermine collar, but that's another story.)

Anyway, luckily we managed to stop Wellington's rascally descendant from stealing everything. When Her Majesty, the present Queen, found out what happened, she said she'd like to keep all the jewels at the Tower for people to look at, if that was all right with us, and give Lord Lambchop some money to help save the jungle cats. We said that was fine, but we'd like to be part of history, and Her Majesty said we already were, and that she'd make sure all the guidebooks about London have me and Minty in them from now on. She has also invited Minty and me to afternoon tea at Buckingham Palace to say thank you. I shall definitely be taking my feathered hat!

Ermine xx

Grand Duchess Maria Von Schnitzel

The Imperial House of Hasbeen

Hasbeen Castle

Balaclavia

Europe

To Flora, for accompanying me
to the Lambeth Palace Gardens
Fete and to Alice, for being
incredibly determined. Jennifer

To Nicolò,
for a new life in the UK
together with our five pets.
Elisa

This collection first published in America in 2020 by Usborne Publishing Ltd., Usborne House, 83-85 Saffron Hill, London EC1N 8RT, England. Usborne.com

Trouble in New York: Text copyright © Jennifer Gray, 2018
Illustrations by Elisa Paganelli © Usborne Publishing Ltd., 2018
Sydney Superstar: Text copyright © Jennifer Gray, 2018 (originally published as *Stoat on Stage*)
Illustrations by Elisa Paganelli © Usborne Publishing Ltd., 2018
The Big London Treasure Hunt: Text copyright © Jennifer Gray, 2019
Illustrations by Elisa Paganelli © Usborne Publishing Ltd., 2019

UK ISBN *Trouble in New York:* 9781474958325 / UK ISBN *Stoat on Stage:* 9781474927260 / UK ISBN *The Big London Treasure Hunt:* 9781474958325
First published in America in 2020, AE, EDC, Tulsa, Oklahoma 74146
www.usbornebooksandmore.com

American ISBN: 9780794549046
ALB ISBN: 9781601304933
JFMAMJ ASOND/20 05771/2
Printed in Dongguan, Guangdong, China.